THE BREAKUP BROKER

AN EVER AFTER NOVEL

KELLY COLLINS

CHAPTER ONE

Savvy

The trick to breaking hearts professionally is to convince yourself you never had one to begin with. And on most days, that was almost true.

This morning, for example, I tapped the fishbowl on my dresser with all the enthusiasm of a DMV employee. "Breakup number three hundred and forty-two, Commitment. Wish me luck." My beta fish flared his fins, either oblivious to the irony of his name or fully in on the joke. His glassy stare offered more warmth than my first coffee of the day.

But today, there was a spark of something—something I wasn't supposed to feel. Guilt? Regret? I shoved it down the way I always did. People didn't hire me for my emotions. They hired me to finish what they couldn't.

The business had grown entirely through whispered referrals in Manhattan's elite circles—private clubs, charity galas, and corporate boardrooms. My clients found me through an intricate network of satisfied customers and their therapists, each passing along my private business number—unlisted, unadvertised, and shared only through whispers of trust. No website, no social media, no paper trail. Just the promise of a clean break delivered with professional precision.

The scent of coffee drifted up from River Bend Books as my mom started the day below. Light pooled across the train schedule taped to my mirror—a sharp, daily reminder: seventy-five minutes to New York, which meant just over an hour to heartbreak duty.

Commitment swam lazy loops in his bowl. Some days, I envied how simple it must be to live in a world that small. I'd tried explaining to my mother that I hadn't named him as some deep metaphor about my love life, or aversion to one—but the pet store frowned on me naming him Sushi.

Still, whenever love or relationships came up, she'd given me that same sad look since I'd turned down my dream job at Windsor Weddings to become what she called a "professional relationship undertaker."

My mom had been married to my dad for thirty-two years—the only thing she'd ever known was true love. To her, my career choice was like swapping a fairy-tale ending for a eulogy.

I tried not to think about what that said about me.

My phone buzzed. Today's client number and the bare minimum details.

CLIENT #342

Navy suit, grande dark roast. Meet at Rise and Grind Coffee at 9 a.m.

Simple enough. But simple didn't mean easy. One wrong word and a breakup could spiral out of control—into legal battles, public meltdowns, or, worst of all, bad press.

The breakup broker business didn't have Yelp reviews, but my reputation relied on word of mouth. A single mistake could put me out of work faster than you could say "amicable split."

The floorboards creaked their morning greeting as I crossed to my closet. My collection of breakup outfits hung in neat rows, organized by the type of heartbreak they delivered. Power suits for corporate types, business casual for startup bros, and one very specific blazer I saved for trust fund babies who thought their father's money made them unbreakable.

"Going with the navy today," I told Commitment, who showed his approval by continuing to swim in circles. "Nothing says 'your girlfriend hired me to dump you' like a sensible blazer and practical pumps."

The bell downstairs chimed as the first customer entered the bookstore. My mom's voice, warm as fresh coffee, greeted Mrs. Patterson, who always showed up before the official open time, undoubtedly wanting to know if her latest book order had arrived. The morning ritual of River Bend was as predictable as my own—unlike the city, where chaos was just a coffee order away from erupting.

My phone lit up with the group chat.

IVY

EMERGENCY. The bride just fired her actual best friend. I need a backstory for being a camp counselor FIVE years ago. Help.

MADDY

Again? Last week, you were a college roommate. How many lives are you living?

IVY

> Seven. No, eight. I lost count after the twins' wedding, where I had to be two different bridesmaids.

ME

> At least you're creating happy endings. My calendar says "soul crushing" at nine.

MADDY

> We covered the whole love cycle, didn't we? I plan the perfect proposal, and Ivy gets them down the aisle. Then Savvy...

IVY

> Handles the ones who don't make it. The Three Fates of Manhattan Romance.

ME

> I'm pretty sure this isn't what we meant when planning our "perfect wedding empire" in college.

MADDY

> Maybe not. But at least we're still in it together. Different corners of the same business.

The familiar rhythm of our banter almost made me forget what I was about to do. Almost. But even after all those breakups, it hadn't made this one any easier.

I grabbed my bag, checked my lipstick—neutral, professional, absolutely not the same shade I wore during my heartbreak—and headed for the side entrance. During store hours, I could cut through the back storage room and take the interior stairs down, but the exterior staircase was faster when the shop wasn't open.

I slipped outside, avoiding the romance display I could see my mother arranging through the window. Three hundred and forty-one breakups later, I still couldn't look at those promises of forever without flinching.

The scent of damp leaves and river water hung in the air, crisp with the first hints of autumn.

Mrs. Patterson had left and was now entering the post office, probably updating Frank about the latest town gossip. Old Mr. Dixon was unlocking The Weathered Barn, though why he bothered when nothing ever sold was one of River Bend's greatest mysteries.

My phone buzzed again.

MADDY

Drone rehearsal moved to 2. Had to promise the parks department no water features this time.

IVY

Still need that camp counselor backstory! How do you feel about archery?

ME

Heading to the train. Try not to create any more true love while I'm crushing someone's dreams.

MADDY

That's our Savvy. Bringing balance to the universe, one broken heart at a time.

The train station sat at the edge of town like a postcard from 1952. Complete with a copper-green roof and more gingerbread trim than a Christmas cookie, it served as both a transportation hub and an unofficial town museum. The walls were lined with black-and-white photos of River Bend's brushes with fame—FDR's whistle-stop campaign, that time Grace Kelly's car broke down and Dad's grandfather fixed it at the shop, and the summer they filmed

Autumn in New York using Main Street as a backdrop. The town council still argued whether Richard Gere ate at Common Grounds or just stood outside.

"Morning, Savvy." Tom, who'd been selling train tickets since before I was born, waved from his booth. "Another Wednesday, another broken heart?"

"Just doing my part to keep the therapists of New York employed." I tapped my monthly pass against the reader. The Metropolitan Transit Authority might have gone digital, but Tom's booth still had the original brass ticket window, polished daily by his proud hands.

The 7:15 whistle cut through the morning air, right on schedule. Joe, the conductor, had the door to my usual car open, and sure enough, there was my seat—the one that mysteriously remained empty every day I traveled, complete with a fresh box of tissues tucked into the magazine pocket. I'd tried asking Joe once how the seat remained unoccupied, but he just gave me that all-too-familiar smile and handed me a peppermint.

"One of these days," Joe said as I settled in, "you're going to get on this train looking like someone who hasn't memorized every sad song Taylor Swift ever wrote."

"I'll have you know I've branched out to Adele." I pulled out my phone, rechecking the morning's client details. I never asked for names or contact information, just time, place, and basic identification markers. Today was simple.

The train rolled past River Bend's greatest hits—the gazebo where Maddy still tested all her proposal ideas, the park where Ivy had coordinated her first wedding party photos, the bench where I … well, some landmarks were better left in the past.

New York was big. Too big for chance encounters. At

least, that's what I told myself. Still, after all these years, I was surprised I'd never run into Henry. Eight million people, yet the city could feel impossibly small when it wanted to. Maybe it was because he lived in a different world now—a world of gala dinners, designer suits, and family mergers. Meanwhile, I'd traded one kind of small town for another, choosing bookstores over boardrooms and freedom over expectations. I wasn't sure if that made me brave or just lonely.

Through the window, I watched my small town transform into increasingly urban landscapes, like a flip book of everything I was leaving behind. River Bend, where everyone knew your name, your coffee order, and exactly which NYU boy had ghosted you into a career change. The city, where anonymity was just another luxury item, like oat milk or therapy.

My phone buzzed with updates from the morning's disasters in progress.

IVY

CRISIS. Bride's real camp friend just posted a photo from the actual camp. I need a new backstory ASAP.

MADDY

Tell them you were at a sister camp across the lake.

IVY

There was no lake.

ME

Say you were the kid of the archery instructor who worked in town. No one remembers the townies.

The train lurched toward Grand Central Station, the

skyline rising like jagged promises on the horizon. I straightened my blazer and prepared to become Jennifer. Using another name was part of the job. A layer of separation. Jennifer Walsh handled the messy parts of love, so Savvy Honeysucker didn't have to.

At least, that's how it was supposed to work. The city was big enough that I should feel safe, invisible. But every so often, I wondered what would happen if someone—if *he* —recognized me. The thought tightened around my ribs like a trap. One wrong step, and everything I'd worked so hard to compartmentalize could come crashing down.

CHAPTER TWO

Savvy

Rise and Grind Coffee took pretentious coffee culture to new heights. It was all exposed brick and twenty-dollar avocado toast. Their menu board looked like a chemistry experiment gone wrong, with drinks that required a PhD to pronounce. But they served the best-overpriced coffee in Manhattan, which made them the perfect spot for delivering bad news to people who treated their morning order like a TED talk.

I claimed my strategic corner spot—another lesson learned from years of experience. Like real estate, it was location, location, location. The corner table offered clear sight lines to both exits, acoustic privacy from the espresso machine's screech, and just enough witnesses to prevent anything too dramatic. Plus, the leather banquette meant no risk of pins-and-needles legs at crucial moments.

I'd learned that one the hard way. During my first month on the job, I'd chosen one of those Instagram-worthy cafés where the furniture was designed for photos, not function. Try maintaining professional dignity while your foot's asleep and you're perched on a wobbly metal stool that could double as modern art. The client had cried. I'd stumbled when I tried to stand, and we'd both ended up wearing his artisanal cold brew.

Now, I had a mental map of every decent meeting spot in Manhattan. This corner at Rise and Grind Coffee was my favorite—good coffee, better sight lines, and actual chairs designed for sitting. A true professional never lets furniture interfere with their performance.

As I settled into my seat, the morning crowd flowed around me, each table offering a glimpse into relationships at every conceivable stage. A couple by the window was definitely on the rocks—he kept checking his phone under the table while she stirred her coffee like she was trying to create a whirlpool that would sweep her away.

At the bar, a woman in yoga pants was negotiating a drink order with more substitutions than a high-stakes contract while FaceTiming her therapist. It was just another Wednesday in Manhattan, where therapy sessions were less about privacy and more like a badge of status—loud enough for everyone in a ten-foot radius to overhear.

My phone lit up with another group chat.

MADDY

The proposal guy asked if we could train squirrels to carry the ring.

ME

Better than pigeons.

MADDY

That was ONE TIME. And they were doves.

IVY

For the first time in years, the bride wants me to be in chartreuse. CHARTREUSE. With ruffles. And a bustle.

ME

At least my uniform is reusable. I've crushed over a hundred dreams in this same blue blazer. Got to go. Client meeting in five. See you tonight.

I tucked my phone away as the café's morning rush hit its peak. Nine o'clock approached, and I pulled out my Jennifer Walsh business cards, straightened my blazer, and waited. In exactly three minutes, I would decide if this job called for my sympathetic head tilt or my professional nod of understanding.

The bell above the door chimed. Right on schedule, Navy Suit walked in. His Manhattan blend of confidence and coffee snobbery became the standard issue with an MBA and a trust fund.

It was almost funny how I'd ended up here. After Henry, I'd tried everything to forget—dove into wedding planning with Maddy and Ivy, threw myself into business school applications, and even interviewed at Windsor Weddings. But every happy couple was a mockery, every promise of forever like a time bomb. Then, one day, I over- heard a woman at Common Grounds trying to figure out how to end things with her fiancé. The words had tumbled out before I could stop them. "I'll do it for you." When I said I would deliver her goodbye, the relief on her face was like looking in a mirror. Somehow, helping others end things cleanly had become my way of giving others what I never got—closure.

I lifted my hand in the practiced Jennifer Walsh

gesture—not too eager, just the right amount of corporate polish. "Over here," I called out. "Thank you for meeting with me."

Navy Suit slid into the seat across from me, all straight white teeth and misplaced confidence. "Jennifer." He extended his hand. "Thanks for taking the time. My team has put together some projections I think you'll find impressive."

He was deep into page three of his market analysis, pitching me hard on projected returns, when I held up a hand. "I'm going to stop you right there."

He blinked, surprised, his pen hovering above an annotated chart.

"When your girlfriend asked you to meet me, it was under the guise of a vetted client for an investment proposal." I leaned in, keeping my voice calm but direct. "But I'm here for something else."

His brows knit in confusion. "What ... what is this about? If not for this, why did Rachel set up this meeting?"

I kept my expression neutral, maintaining a calm professionalism. "Rachel? I know her as client #342."

The color drained from his face. "Wait ... what is this about?"

"She feels that your relationship has run its course. You two are more of a habit than a love match. I'm here to tell you that while she cares about you, she no longer wants to continue the relationship."

He blinked, clearly caught off guard, so I added gently, "You're married—to your job. And she's not looking to play second fiddle to your career. She wants something real, something with balance. And that's not what she's experienced with you."

The words landed like a punch, and he took a sharp

breath, gripping his portfolio until his knuckles turned white. "She hired someone to break up with me?"

"Sometimes a little distance provides clarity," I said, each word polished from repetition. It was the kindest way to deliver the blow.

He stared at me, trying to make sense of it all. "Like ... an emotional contractor?" His voice dripped with disbelief.

I'd heard variations of that question a hundred times, but the way he cataloged me like some kind of outsourced feelings manager was almost funny.

"This is insane." He yanked at his tie as if it were suddenly strangling him. "You ... you do this for a living?"

"Yes, I provide a service." My voice stayed steady even as my heart did its usual twist. "A clean break, delivered with respect."

He scoffed, his eyes narrowing. "Respect? Sending someone else to do your dirty work? That's not respect—that's cowardice."

The word hit like a slap. *Cowardice.* Was that really what this was? Maybe. But it was still better than unanswered texts, ghosted calls, and the hollow silence where a goodbye should have been. I'd seen the damage that it did—how it could tear someone apart, how it had torn *me* apart. Henry Kingston and I discussed marriage and babies one day, mapping our future together. And then he was gone, like a chapter ripped out of a book. No goodbye, no explanation. Just silence. Even if this job was messy, at least it was a form of closure people could hold on to—something I'd never gotten.

"She's packed your things," I said, choosing my words. "They'll be with the doorman by noon. She's asked for no contact."

He stood so abruptly his chair scraped against the floor.

Several heads turned our way, but I kept my expression neutral. Rule number six: never let them see you sweat.

"You must hate love," he said, his words laced with resentment.

Then he turned and walked away, his portfolio clutched tightly in his hand.

His words shouldn't have stung—I'd heard worse. Last week, someone called me a joy-killing succubus, and for a split second, I considered slapping it on my business cards. But this? This was different.

No. I didn't hate love. I hated what happened when it was abandoned without a goodbye. I hated the unanswered questions, the sleepless nights wondering what went wrong. I hated how silence could carve someone up, leaving them raw and unfinished. I hated how people turned their backs on it, leaving destruction in their wake.

My phone buzzed.

CLIENT #342

Did he take it okay?

I didn't respond. That wasn't part of the service. Clean breaks meant clean breaks all around.

The train ride home stretched ahead of me like an emotional gauntlet. At least I had wine night to look forward to. Nothing soothed the ache of other people's broken hearts quite like watching Maddy brainstorm increasingly absurd proposal ideas and listening to Ivy justify why she needed a crash course in flower arranging by Saturday.

I just had to make it through the crying portion of my commute first.

Joe was waiting at my usual spot, a tissue box in my seat. "Rough one?"

"He called me a contractor for feelings." I slid into my designated space, the one with the conveniently placed window for staring dramatically at the passing scenery.

"Could be worse. Remember the guy who tried to hire you to break up with his wife?"

"That's not a thing I do." I pulled out the first tissue. "Also, pretty sure that's just called divorce."

The city fell away behind us as I worked through my post-breakup ritual. Five minutes of actual crying, ten minutes of wondering if I was helping anyone or just spreading misery like an emotional pyramid scheme, and the rest of the ride to put my River Bend face back on.

My phone lit up again.

MADDY

911—Need someone to test the proposal setup. The city denied my permit for releasing doves.

IVY

They're still mad about the pigeon incident?

MADDY

THEY WERE DOVES!

MADDY

I need someone to stand in the right spot so I can practice the drones' timing.

IVY

NO MORE DRONES.

MADDY

These are different drones! With better GPS!

ME

Like the ones that spelled out "Hairy Mole?" instead of "Marry Me?"

MADDY

I hate you both. Also, is wine night still on?

ME

After today? I'll need two bottles.

CORK & Crown was bustling when I walked in, the Wednesday night crowd in full swing. Gloria Chen, River Bend's owner—and Maddy's mom—spotted me and started pulling my usual bottle before I even reached the bar. With her cozy sweaters, blunt humor, and lifelong ties to River Bend, Gloria was hardly the type you'd expect to own a trendy wine bar, but she somehow made it feel both chic and unpretentious.

"That bad, huh?" Gloria's gaze settled on my smudged mascara. "And those eyes..." She tilted her head, studying me. "Remember when they were that electric blue? Like summer lightning? Now they're more overcast—like the sky just before the rain breaks. And your hair..." Her lips curved, just barely. "Used to be that rich chestnut, but now? It's looking a little like the River Bend mud banks after a flood."

"My eyes are the same as they've always been." I gripped the glass she had just poured like a lifeline.

Gloria's expression grew tender. "I'll send some of my conditioning treatment home with Maddy. I can fix your hair, sweetheart. The rest?" She caught my gaze in the mirrored backsplash and held it there, her voice gentler now. "That sparkle will come back when you're ready. Must've been a rough day."

I sank onto my usual stool with a long sigh. "Could've been worse. At least I didn't end up wearing his coffee."

Gloria chuckled and topped off my glass. "On the house. You look like you need it."

Ivy burst through the door in a swirl of tulle and urgency, her honey-blonde hair escaping its twist to create a halo in the bar's dim lighting. She was all delicate features and perpetual motion, like one of those Disney princesses come to life—if Disney princesses regularly committed identity fraud for bridezillas. "Does anyone know how to say, 'I caught the bouquet at your sister's wedding' in Swedish?"

I raised an eyebrow. "Why would you need to know that?"

She sighed, sliding onto the stool beside me. "Bride's orders. I'm now her childhood friend from Stockholm, fluent in Swedish, and allergic to shellfish. If they serve two-pound lobsters for dinner and I have to miss it, I'm going to be pissed. Lobster is my favorite."

Maddy arrived next, juggling what looked suspiciously like drone remote controls. She had her mother's elegant features and glossy black hair—currently pulled into a messy bun—but where Gloria moved like a gentle stream, Maddy was all crashing waves, her tall frame making the delicate remote controls look like children's toys in her hands.

"Before either of you say anything, these drones are foolproof. Perfect spelling, zero chance of a mishap."

"Good to know," Gloria said, setting out two more glasses with a smirk. "Nothing like last time, then?"

"Different," Maddy assured us, setting the controls down. "They've got GPS and anti-bird tech—the works."

Gloria topped off our glasses, then leaned against the bar. "So, Savvy, how many hearts did you crush today?"

"Just one." I shrugged. "But he didn't take it well."

Ivy winced. "Those are the worst. The ones who get all dramatic about it."

"Or try to make it about you," Maddy added.

"Or ask for second chances." Gloria shook her head, chuckling. "Classic mistake."

Maddy brightened suddenly, reaching for her bag. "Speaking of classic mistakes, what do we think about skywriting? Because I have this new client—"

"NO," Ivy and I said in unison.

"You haven't even heard the whole idea!"

"Does it involve anything that could fall from the sky?" I asked.

"Or spell out unfortunate messages?" Ivy added.

"Or attract birds?" Gloria chimed in.

Maddy deflated. "You all lack vision."

"And you lack basic pattern recognition," I pointed out. "Remember the hot air balloon incident?"

"That restraining order was dropped," she muttered into her wine.

My phone buzzed with a new client alert. Friday, nine a.m. Rise and Grind Coffee again. Tall, blue suit. Another day, another navy suit. In Manhattan, that was about as specific as saying, "He has hair."

"Another one so soon?" Ivy peered at my screen. "That's unusual for you."

"Bills don't pay themselves." I tucked my phone away.

"You know what you need?" Maddy set down her glass

with the particular emphasis that meant she was about to suggest something terrible. "A website."

"No."

"Just hear me out—"

"Absolutely not."

"You could call it 'It's Not Me, It's You.com!'"

Ivy choked on her wine. "Or 'Honeysucker's Heart Removal Service.'"

"'Got Ghosted? Ghost Better!'" Gloria offered.

"I hate all of you." I reached for the bottle. "And I'm not advertising. Word of mouth works just fine."

"To tomorrow." Gloria raised her glass one last time. "May your drones fly straight—"

"They will!" Maddy interjected.

"Your Swedish accent hold up—"

"Jag är mycket svensk!" Ivy attempted.

"And your heart..." Gloria looked at me. "Someday, break free of that wall you've built."

After we split the bill, I gathered my things to head home. The walk from Cork & Crown took precisely six minutes, long enough for River Bend's evening soundtrack of crickets to clear my head.

October had transformed the sugar maples lining Main Street into torches of red and gold, while Storm King Mountain stood silhouetted against the harvest moon across the dark water. Old Mrs. Patterson's porch light cast a warm glow across her rocking chair, empty now but still swaying in the night breeze. As I approached home, the "Closed" sign in River Bend Books' window glowed softly, my mom's neat handwriting visible beneath it: *Tomorrow's another chapter.*

CHAPTER THREE

Henry

"It's time, son." My father poured three fingers of scotch at the bar tucked into the corner of his study, another Thursday ritual as old as my failures. "The Ashworths have been more than patient."

I stood at the wall of windows overlooking Central Park West, twenty stories up in the building where doormen knew your coffee order and residents had private elevator banks. The park was painted in shades of gold and red—like the trees that lined Main Street in River Bend.

No. I couldn't think about her. Not now. Not when my father expected answers I didn't have.

"Caroline's a fine match." The crystal decanter clinked against the glass with precise, measured strikes. Like everything else about Richard Kingston III, the sound conveyed power. "Her family's wealth nearly rivals ours. Nearly." He let the word hang in the air, thick with judgment. In my world, that minor distinction meant everything.

I turned from the window, his words pulling me back

toward the armchair by the fireplace. The leather creaked as I sat, the air heavy with the scent of old scotch and older expectations.

Every inch of the study reminded anyone who entered that the Kingstons had never been more powerful. It was a room built to command respect and suppress rebellion.

I'd learned that lesson the hard way. I hadn't fought for her—not when it mattered most. And the worst part was knowing that I should have. It had been a lifetime since I'd seen her, yet Savvy lingered in every corner of my mind.

She was nothing like the polished, predictable women my father paraded before me—Caroline included. Savvy had been a hurricane. Uncontrollable, vibrant, and far too dangerous for the Kingston legacy.

My gaze flicked to the portrait of my grandfather above the marble fireplace. Richard Kingston Sr., patriarch and architect of the Kingston empire, looked out with cold eyes that seemed to say, *You don't get to choose. None of us ever did.*

"You've been dodging this for weeks, Henry." My father poured a precise measure of scotch into another crystal glass and handed it to me. "The Ashworths won't wait forever. You need to plan."

I swirled the amber liquid in my glass, staring into its depths as if it held answers.

"This isn't about what you want," he continued, his voice sharp. "The Kingston name is bigger than you, bigger than me. Choice isn't part of the deal. That's the price of privilege."

The pressure of those expectations pressed down harder in the study, where the air seemed thick with ambition and legacy.

I leaned back in the leather armchair, closing my eyes. I

could still hear her laugh, the way she'd said my name like it wasn't tied to generations of obligation. Sometimes, I wondered if she'd forgotten me entirely—or if she still carried the broken pieces of our relationship.

The glass of scotch sat untouched in my hand, a reminder of the legacy I couldn't escape and the life I couldn't have.

Those distinctions stared down at me from the walls—four generations of Kingston men captured in oils, each portrait more imposing than the last. Great-great-grandfather Theodore, who'd built our first bank. Great-grandfather Richard I, who'd turned it into an empire. My father's father, Richard II, who'd merged us into the billion-dollar stratosphere with real estate. They all have those ice-blue Kingston eyes, watching, judging, expecting.

"The Kingston legacy demands certain … standards." He lifted his glass toward Theodore's portrait. "Certain responsibilities. You have to marry, son. And soon. Statistically speaking, the longer you wait to have children, the more likely you will have a girl." He gestured to the wall of portraits. "Two hundred years of Kingston men. Don't screw that up because you can't do what's expected of you."

My stomach turned. "I wanted to marry once. Remember how that worked out?"

"Don't tell me you're still—" He lowered his glass hard enough to slosh the amber liquid over the edge. "For God's sake, Henry. It's been five years. Let it go."

Five years, two months, and thirteen days. Not that I was counting.

"The Honeysuckers," he spat the name like a curse, "would never fit into our world. The Kingstons have married Vanderbilts, Carnegies, and Astors. We don't marry

... Honeysuckers." He laughed, cruel and sharp. "Lord, how does one even become a Honeysucker?"

The name hit me like a physical blow, bringing with it the memory of Savvy's laugh as she'd told me the story. We'd been in her family's garage at the marina, watching her father work on Mrs. Patterson's ancient Volvo while the scent of salt and motor oil filled the air. He worked on cars and boats there, the space cluttered with everything from rusted-out engines to half-finished skiffs.

I turned to my father. "Honigsucher," I said, the word foreign but familiar on my tongue. "They were beekeepers in Germany. It means honey seekers—before Ellis Island got creative with the spelling—"

"I don't need a history lesson on peasant surnames." My father's voice sliced through the air. "I need you to do your duty to this family. Caroline's father called again this morning."

I swallowed the scotch, letting it burn. "I'm meeting Caroline for coffee tomorrow."

"Coffee?" He barked out a laugh. "You're not meeting her for coffee, you're meeting her to propose. It's time, Henry. Past time." He moved to the portrait wall, straightening a frame that didn't need straightening. "The merger documents are ready. The press release is drafted. All you need is the ring."

"You mean the ring is all you require."

"Watch yourself." His voice dropped to that dangerous register I remembered from childhood. "I've been more than patient with your ... reluctance. But the Ashworths won't wait forever. Do you think you're the only suitable match for Caroline?"

"Maybe she should find someone who loves her."

He turned, those Kingston-blue eyes piercing right

through me. "Love? Is that what you think you had with that mechanic's daughter? That little dreamer who thought she could build a wedding business with her equally delusional friends?"

The memory of Savvy's dreams twisted in my chest. She'd had it all planned—the three of them spreading happiness across New York, one wedding at a time. I'd also believed in that dream until my father had made his plans crystal clear.

"One phone call to the building department, Henry. That's all it would take. Their quaint little bookstore would be buried in violations—safety hazards, code infractions, structural concerns. They'd be shut down before they could even file an appeal. And the marina? I buy that property, raise the rent on Paul's repair shop, and just like that—her family loses everything. Their businesses, their future—gone in an instant. It'd be a rounding error in our quarterly report."

I'd made my choice that night. Walked away. Disappeared from her life without a word. Because the alternative —watching my father systematically destroy her family— would have killed me. Better to break her heart quickly than watch her world crumble piece by piece.

"You made the right choice then." My father's voice pulled me back to the present, reading my thoughts with that unnerving precision he possessed. "I was proud of you that day."

"You didn't give me much choice." The words sat heavy on my tongue, dry and bitter, like ash after a fire.

"I gave you exactly the choice you needed." He moved to the wall, swinging aside a portrait to reveal the safe. "And I still do. Don't forget that."

The safe door swung open with a whisper of expensive

engineering. My father reached inside and pulled out a black velvet box that screamed old money and older expectations.

"A five-carat cushion cut." He opened the box, letting the diamond catch the light. "Both family crests are engraved inside the band."

My stomach lurched. This wasn't just a ring—it was a collar, perfectly sized and waiting. "You bought an engagement ring without telling me?"

"I made an investment in our future." He held the box out like a challenge. "The future you're going to secure tomorrow morning."

All I could think about was the ring I'd picked out for Savvy five years ago. It was vintage, warm rose gold that reminded me of sunset on the Hudson and a stone that sparkled like her eyes when she laughed. I'd spent months searching for something as unique as she was.

"The Ashworths expect the announcement by week's end." He set the box on his desk with the finality that had crushed better men than me. "Their PR team is coordinating with ours. Caroline's father and I agree—the Four Seasons, an intimate dinner, a handpicked guest list. The society papers will eat it up."

"And if I say no?"

His expression could have frozen hell. "Then I make that call. How long do you think Paul Honeysucker can keep his family afloat once I own that marina? How many books can they sell when that Victorian gets condemned?" He leaned forward, hands flat on the desk. "And you? How far will you get in this industry when I blacklist you? The Kingston name cuts both ways, son. It can open doors—or slam them shut forever."

Five years and nothing had changed. He still held all the power, and we both knew it.

I snatched the ring box off his desk, shoving it into my pocket as I stormed out. My mother stood in the hallway, elegant as always in Chanel, looking like she'd been waiting. Maybe she had been—she'd developed a sixth sense over the years for when these father-son chats went nuclear. She'd been doing this dance for years, standing in hallways, smoothing over Richard's ultimatums, trying to protect me the only way she could—with quiet warnings and timed interventions. She was the first to notice Savvy's effect on me, the one who lit up when I brought home books from River Bend, and the one who told me once that some things were worth more than the Kingston name.

"Henry." She touched my arm. "Don't let him—"

"How do you do it, Mom?" The words came out rougher than I intended. "How do you stand being married to him?"

A shadow passed her eyes—fear, resignation, years of careful compromises. "We all make our choices, darling." She straightened my tie, a nervous habit from my childhood. "Don't forget to visit your grandfather this week. He's having more good days than bad lately, but..." She didn't finish the thought. She didn't have to.

James Morrison might have built his own fortune in real estate, but all the money in Manhattan couldn't slow what was happening to his mind. Still, on his good days, he was the only one who'd ever truly understood me.

"I'll stop by tomorrow." I kissed her cheek, catching the familiar scent of Chanel No. 5. "After I meet with Caroline."

As I rode down in the private elevator, the ring box felt heavier with every passing second. Even the doorman's deferential nod added to the pressure settling over me. Outside, Central Park stretched across the street, its trees blazing under the October sunset like nature's version of stained glass—so different from River Bend, where autumn's colors reflected off the Hudson, making the entire world glow.

Tomorrow morning's coffee meeting loomed ahead. Caroline wanted to discuss weekend plans at Rise and Grind Coffee—not one of our usual Upper East Side spots. A root canal would be preferable. Hell, another lecture from my father would be better.

Not that Caroline was awful. By any standard, she was a catch—educated student at Yale, striking in that cool Nordic way and impeccably connected—the woman who looked perfect in society photos and knew exactly which fork to use at state dinners.

But there was nothing when I was with her—no spark, flutter, or dizzying rush. I suspected she felt the same. We were two perfectly matched pieces of a puzzle neither of us wanted to complete.

Savvy was the opposite of everything Caroline represented. Caroline was a perfectly cut gem, polished and predictable. Savvy was fire and warmth—imperfect and wild in all the ways I hadn't known I needed until I lost her.

A memory hit me so hard that I had to stop walking. Savvy, perched on a coffeehouse couch during finals week, planning her future wedding business with Maddy and Ivy. The three of them were so full of dreams and determination. I'd looked them up once, in a moment of weakness—or masochism. Ivy had become some professional bridesmaid if her Instagram was to be believed. Maddy's LinkedIn listed her as a "Romance Logistics Specialist," whatever that meant. But Savvy? She'd vanished completely as if she'd never existed. No social media, no business listings, nothing. Maybe that was for the best. Now here I was, five years later, with an engagement ring I didn't want and less than twenty-four hours to determine how to use it.

I needed a drink—several, actually—but first I had to call my grandfather's nurse, then figure out how the hell I was going to face tomorrow with this ring pressing against me like a bad decision.

The irony wasn't lost on me. I'd walked away from Savvy to save her future, and now I was walking into a proposal to secure mine.

Tomorrow, I'd seal my father's deal—with a ring I didn't want, to a woman I never loved, for a life I didn't want to live.

CHAPTER FOUR

Savvy

The message hit my phone at 7:42 a.m. as I walked to my usual spot on the train platform. The October morning air had that particular River Bend crispness that usually centered me before a job. Not today. My stomach lurched at the words on my screen.

> CLIENT #343
>
> He'll be early. He thinks we're discussing weekend plans.

I read it three times, and each word landed like a punch. No elaborate setup? No careful fiction about investment opportunities or career mentoring? Just ... weekend plans? In my years of professional heartbreaking, I'd never gone in this naked.

This wasn't just another job—this was sloppy. And sloppy meant risk. Risk to my reputation, control, and the walls I'd built between work and life.

The morning spun further out of control when Joe

wasn't at his usual spot by my car door. Instead, a harried-looking man I'd never seen before announced that Joe was out sick. My seat—the one that mysteriously stayed empty every morning—was occupied by a man in wireless head-phones who took up more than his fair share of space.

The familiar seventy-five-minute ride stretched ahead of me without my usual tissue-box safety net. *Perfect.*

My phone vibrated again. A message from my client, #343:

CLIENT #343

> I'm tailing him now. He's wearing a navy Armani suit and should sit at the corner booth.

I clutched my phone tighter, anxiety climbing with each mile marker. This wasn't how I operated. I needed those precious pre-meeting moments to prepare to transform from River Bend Savvy to Jennifer, a professional heartbreaker.

I burst out of Grand Central at 9:17, the usual pre-game confidence that steadied me replaced by a gnawing dread that carried the sharp edge of guilt. Rise and Grind Coffee's morning rush was in full swing, the line for coffee snaking out the door. My strategic corner booth was hidden behind the crowd. Another disruption to my careful routine.

When I made it inside, fresh espresso mingled with vanilla and cinnamon. Usually, this was comforting—a ritual that marked the beginning of another job—but today the aroma made my stomach churn.

Two men in navy suits occupied the corner window tables, and I didn't know which was my mark. For the first time in years, I'd have to slide in as the guest, not the host.

I snapped a quick photo, my hands shaking enough to blur the first attempt.

ME

Which one?

The response came instantly.

CLIENT #343

Right side.

Marcus caught my eye from behind the counter. My favorite barista raised an eyebrow in our usual silent code. *Need backup?*

I shook my head. Marcus had witnessed enough of my "meetings" to read the signs. The sharp click of my heels against hardwood sounded like a countdown to detonation.

The mark's broad shoulders filled his suit with the practiced ease of old money. Something about how he held himself tugged at my memory—a ghost of familiarity that sent an unwelcome shiver down my spine. His fingers drummed against the coffee cup in a rhythm I knew too well. But that was impossible. He was just another client, another navy suit in a city full of them.

I approached, hating this new angle, this loss of control. "I'm so sorry I'm late. The train was—"

He turned, and my practiced script died in my throat. Kingston-blue eyes met mine—and the color drained from our faces. Five years vanished between one heartbeat and the next, leaving me dizzy with the force of remembering. The familiar scent of his cologne slammed into me, yanking me straight back in time.

My legs wobbled as I lowered myself into what should have been my power seat. Every layer of armor I'd painstakingly built buckled under the sheer force of his presence. This was all wrong. I wasn't Savvy Honeysucker right now —I was the breakup broker, the queen of clean exits.

But staring at him, it seemed like that polished persona was slipping away. I wasn't the confident professional I'd trained myself to be. I was twenty-two again, back in River Bend, letting Henry Kingston trace constellations on my skin while the Hudson lapped against the dock. I couldn't be that girl again. Not here. Not now. The familiar scent of his cologne, unchanged from those summers, hit me like a freight train. My stomach twisted, and I gripped the edge of the table to keep from bolting.

Henry had been the center of every dream I'd let myself believe in back then. He was the boy who'd kissed me on the dock at sunset and whispered promises of forever while fireflies danced around us. And he was the one who'd left me to piece together the ruins of those dreams alone.

"Savvy?" His voice was rough, incredulous. The coffee cup clattered against its saucer, dark liquid sloshing dangerously close to the rim. "What in the … how are you…?"

Hearing my name in his voice hit like the distant rumble of a storm you thought had moved on. His gaze lingered on the freckles on my collarbone—freckles he used to trace with his fingertips under the dim glow of string lights on my parents' porch. No. I couldn't let my mind wander there.

"Your girlfriend," I managed, my voice sounding distant even to my own ears. "She hired me."

The words hung between us like a live wire.

I forced my hands to stay steady as I placed my phone face-down on the table, buying precious seconds to compose myself. I never had to look at client messages during meetings. Never. But seeing Henry sitting there, those eyes watching my every move, had scattered my usually perfect recall.

Just read it. Get through it. End it.

With fingers that shook, I picked up my phone and

pulled up the message, the bright screen swimming before my eyes. "She said, and I quote—" My voice cracked. I cleared my throat and started again. "I refuse to enter a union based on my monetary worth. I deserve more than a marriage built on bank statements and business mergers. I want—" Another breath. "I want to marry for love, not to expand family empires or satisfy parental expectations. I want someone who sees me as more than a corporate asset."

The words were like glass in my mouth, each cutting deeper than the last. But what twisted the knife wasn't the message—it was Henry's response.

I expected anger. Expected hurt. Expected anything but the long exhale that escaped him, his shoulders dropping as if a burden had just been lifted. Relief. Pure, unmistakable relief flooded his features.

He adjusted in his seat, and something slipped from his pocket—a velvet box tumbled to the floor, its dark surface collecting coffee shop dust.

My gaze dropped to the box. Everything I'd dreamed about in my early twenties lay inside that box, everything I'd imagined on those endless summer nights when we'd talk about forever.

I looked back at Henry, tears burning behind my eyes. "You came here to propose?" My voice cracked on the last word. "And she's refusing to marry you."

Something dangerously close to satisfaction twisted through the hurt in my chest. Karma had a cruel sense of humor. Here was Henry Kingston, finally ready to commit, holding out the dream I'd once desperately wanted—only to face the very thing he'd given me—rejection.

His relief vanished. He leaned forward, one hand reaching across the table. "Savvy, it's not what—"

"Don't." The word came out harder than I intended.

Professional. Distant. The tone I reserved for clients trying to negotiate. "You disappeared without a word. You have no right to explain. Not now."

"Please, if you'd just listen—"

"I was willing to listen for years, but that time has passed. You aren't even upset that she's dumping you. You're still the same Henry, the one who could walk away without emotion."

I shoved my phone back into my purse, needing something to do with my hands.

I stood, my legs shaking. Before I could stop myself, I bent down, picked up the box, and opened it. Inside, a flawless diamond sat in pristine platinum, every angle precision-cut, every detail perfect.

"Seems perfect," I said, snapping the box closed and placing it on the table with a soft click. "Like everything else in your world. Flawless. Colorless. Lifeless. Just for show."

I turned to leave, my heels clicking against the hardwood like a countdown. Three steps. Two. One.

"Savvy!" His voice carried over the morning crowd, raw and desperate. A few heads turned.

I didn't look back. I couldn't. Because even now, even after everything, he could still undo me faster than a summer storm.

I burst out of Rise and Grind Coffee. The Paper Crane was right next door. Its window display of handmade stationery and imported journals is usually a calming sight, but today, I barely noticed the artful arrangement as I pushed through the door.

The soft chime of bells overhead was lost in the rush of blood in my ears. The shop clerk glanced up from arranging a display of fountain pens but merely nodded as I made a beeline for the back hall restroom. The lock clicked behind me like a gunshot in the tiny space. My legs gave out, and I slid down the wall to the cold cement floor. My hands shook as I pulled out my phone.

ME

911. Paper Crane bathroom. Henry Kingston. HELP.

I hit send to Ivy and Maddy, then let my head fall back against the wall, counting my breaths like I used to count the cars on the Hudson Line, waiting for my best friends to come and piece me back together. Again.

CHAPTER FIVE

Henry

"The Madison Center," I told Thompson, my voice steadier than it had any right to be. The family driver nodded his practiced discretion, not even registering the slight tremor in my hands as I sank into the back seat.

Years of imagining every way I might run into Savvy again, and somehow "hired by my almost-fiancée to dump me" hadn't made the list.

The ring box sat beside me on the leather seat, a silent accusation. I could still see her face as she'd picked it up from the floor. The way her fingers had trembled before that professional mask slammed back into place. *Flawless. Colorless. Lifeless. It's just for show.*

Her words cut deeper than she knew. She'd looked right at that ring—my father's perfect, soulless choice—and saw exactly what it was. A prop in someone else's production.

The city blurred past my window, but all I could see was how she'd changed. Her chestnut hair was darker now, her blue eyes storm-gray and sharp where they used to sparkle. All that time, I wondered if I'd made the right choice, and now I had my answer in the hardness of her voice when she'd said my name.

Caroline hired her to break up with me. Coincidence? Providence? The pieces started falling into place—that practiced calm in her voice, the way she'd delivered Caroline's words like she'd done this before. Was that what she was now? A professional heartbreaker? How had she gone from an aspiring wedding planner to ... this?

The answer hit me like a physical blow. *Me. This was all because of me.*

All those nights, I'd lay awake wondering what had become of her dreams—the wedding planning business with Maddy and Ivy and the future we'd mapped out on lazy Sunday afternoons. Instead, she'd turned her own heartbreak into ... what? A business? A mission? There'd been glimpses of it—the way she'd started with such professional distance, but then I'd seen her hands shake as she'd checked her phone for Caroline's message, watched her struggle to maintain that careful mask.

I'd knocked her off balance. That much was clear. Made her fumble whatever script she usually followed. But underneath her obvious shock, there'd been something practiced about the setup. How she approached the table, the careful way she'd tried to deliver the news before our shared history had derailed everything.

Thompson cleared his throat softly. "We're here, Mr. Kingston."

Madison Center loomed ahead, all gleaming glass and modern angles, nothing like the Victorian architecture my grandfather had spent his life restoring. He would have hated it—probably hated it on his good days when he remembered to.

My phone buzzed. *Father.* Of course. The news of my failed proposal was probably going through his well-oiled network. I sent it to voicemail, knowing there'd be hell to pay later. But I couldn't handle another lecture about Kingston men and family obligations right now.

I shoved the ring box into my pocket, trying to forget its presence.

"Will you be requiring the car later, sir?" Thompson's question pulled me back to the present.

"No, I'll find my way back." Back to what? My father's ultimatum? The mess I'd made of everyone's lives? The ghost of Savvy's professional mask as she'd delivered someone else's goodbye?

The lobby of Madison Center gave the impression of a hotel desperately trying to conceal its true purpose. Fresh flower arrangements were swapped out every day. Abstract art adorned the walls, chosen for its serene palette. Even the faint lavender fragrance couldn't completely overshadow the telltale scent of a hospital.

"Mr. Kingston." The receptionist's expression was practiced and professional, like Savvy's had been before it cracked. "Your grandfather is having a good morning. He's in his room."

I nodded my thanks and headed for the elevators. The ride to the fifth floor was familiar and unsettling, each passing level a reminder of the uncertain conversations that awaited me. How many times had I taken this journey, steeling myself for the moment my grandfather's eyes would meet mine, recognition wavering or dimming like a faulty bulb?

The hallway stretched before me as the elevator doors slid open, the route to his room ingrained in my muscle memory. My feet carried me forward, each step a silent prayer that today would be one of his good days—that the fog of his illness would recede long enough for us to truly connect, even if only for a moment.

I found his door open, warm October sunlight streaming through the floor-to-ceiling windows overlooking the garden. The room was one of the facility's best suites—a fact my father never failed to mention when discussing the cost. James Morrison sat by the window in his favorite leather chair, watching leaves scatter across the manicured lawn below.

He looked up as I approached, and I held my breath, waiting to see if today's version of my grandfather would remember me.

His faded blue eyes sharpened. "Henry. You look troubled."

A squeeze of emotion gripped my chest at the clarity in his voice. These moments were precious now, appearing and vanishing like the sun between storm clouds. I remained standing, taking in the view of the beautiful gardens below. Fall had painted the ornamental pears in shades of burgundy and gold, while late-blooming hydrangeas added splashes of deep purple beneath. Everything about this place was different—too polished, too perfect, like that ring burning a hole in my pocket.

"How do you always know?" The familiar ache of seeing him here, diminished yet still so present, tangled with the raw edges Savvy's appearance had left behind.

"The same way I know when it's going to rain." He tapped his temple, the gesture so achingly familiar it hurt. "Some things you feel in your bones, even when the bones are old and creaky."

On the side table, familiar faces grinned from silver frames— my parents at their tenth anniversary party, graduation, summers in the Hamptons before his mind slipped. I remembered the day each photo was taken, recalled how he'd stood apart at society events, more comfortable among his beloved buildings than Manhattan's elite. His smile reached his eyes in every frame—something I hadn't managed in years.

"I saw her today." The words tumbled out, dragging years of buried guilt along with them. I sank into the visitor's chair beside him, my hands gripping the arms as if holding on could keep the flood of memories from swallowing me whole.

His attention moved from the garden. "The girl from college?"

My throat tightened. He remembered. Of course, he remembered. He'd been the only one who'd understood what Savvy meant to me, seeing past her last name and small-town roots to recognize something real.

"Yes, Savvy," I said, dragging out each syllable like it hurt—because it did.

"Ah." One simple sound, but it carried volumes of understanding.

"She..." I swallowed hard, trying to force down the irony. "She was hired to break up with me. By Caroline."

His laugh startled me, genuine and warm in a way I rarely heard anymore. "Life has a funny way of bringing things full circle, doesn't it?"

The ring box pressed against my thigh, a constant reminder of everything I'd lost and thrown away. "The day I left her, I broke her, Grandpa." The words scraped my throat like sandpaper. "She's different now. Harder."

"Heartbreak hardens people." My grandfather's gaze sharpened, showing me the man who'd built an empire by seeing what others missed. "Did you ever consider that you should have given her the choice? That she was stronger than you gave her credit for?"

The question hit like a physical blow, forcing the air from my lungs. No, I hadn't. I'd done exactly what my father did—decided for others, convinced I knew best. I'd become everything I'd sworn I'd never be, wielding power like a weapon, thinking I could protect her by controlling her fate.

"You can't abandon something because it's difficult," he said, looking out at the leaves blowing in the wind. "Sometimes the best things in life come from working through the challenges."

I stared past him at those falling leaves, remembering how Savvy used to sit in the bookstore window seat, dreaming up futures that now would never be. The future I'd stolen from her with my silence, my cowardice masked as nobility. "I don't think there's anything left to rebuild." The words seemed hollow, echoing my father's certainty that everything could be reduced to simple profit and loss equations.

"There's always something worth saving." He patted my hand, his touch as familiar as my guilt. "If you know where to look. And if you're willing to do the work."

His words hung in the air as an aide appeared with his morning coffee service. The moment of clarity was ending —I could see it in the way his eyes clouded, like watching a door slowly close. But he'd given me something to hold on to. Even as his mind betrayed him, his heart remained true.

I stood to leave, but his hand caught my sleeve. "Henry?"

"Yes?"

"Some breaks..." He gestured vaguely toward the

garden, where sunlight fractured through autumn leaves. "Some breaks let the light in."

I kissed his forehead, inhaling the familiar scent of his aftershave, wondering how many more lucid moments we had left. How many more chances would I have to hear his wisdom before the fog claimed him completely?

"I should go." I stood, straightening my jacket. "Do you need anything? Books? Music?"

"Bring that girl to visit." His voice carried a surprising strength.

"Grandpa, I can't—that's not possible."

"Anything's possible if you want it bad enough." His eyes held that sharp clarity again. "Humor this old man, Henry. I don't ask for much."

The request coiled around my ribs, squeezing the air from my lungs. He was right—he never asked for anything, not even when they'd moved him here. While my father demanded the world reshape itself to his will, James Morrison accepted life's changes with quiet grace.

"I'll see you soon, Grandpa."

Outside, the October sun painted Manhattan in shades of gold, but I could only see the storm in Savvy's eyes when she'd delivered Caroline's goodbye. My phone buzzed again —probably my father, demanding an update. Instead of answering, I pulled up a different contact and dialed.

"Mason? I need a favor, off the books."

The line crackled momentarily before Mason's steady, deep voice answered. "The last time you asked for an off-the-books favor was that mess in the Caymans."

The Caymans. My jaw tightened at the memory. A too-loud night, too much bourbon, and the reckless spiral that ended in a holding cell. I'd thought I could drink Savvy out of my system and drown her memory in liquor and poor decisions, but it had been impossible. She clung to the corners of my mind, untouchable and relentless, even as I tried to lose myself in the haze.

Mason had been the one to pull me out of it—literally. He'd dragged me from the mess I'd made before it hit the papers, but not before delivering a scathing assessment of my character. He hadn't minced words. "This isn't you, Henry," he'd said. "At least, it didn't used to be."

"I need you to find someone for me," I said, forcing the words past the tightness in my chest. "Savannah Honeysucker."

A sharp intake of breath sounded on the other end of the line. "Jesus, Henry. Your father—"

"That's why this stays between us."

There was a pause, one that seemed heavier than it should have. Mason wasn't a man who hesitated often. His answer came, steady and sure. "Give me an hour."

CHAPTER SIX

Savvy

Like my professional composure, the lock on The Paper Crane's bathroom had seen better days—scratched, tarnished, and barely holding it together. I pressed my forehead against the cool tile wall, counting breaths like Mom taught me when the world got too big. In through the nose, out through the mouth. Repeat until the room stops spinning.

Years of constructed walls were demolished by one pair of blue eyes.

The fluorescent light overhead hummed faintly, the only sound piercing the silence. Time dragged—thirty minutes? Sixty? Over an hour. I couldn't tell. My phone sat untouched in my bag, notifications piling up. I didn't dare look. What would I even say?

I leaned back against the wall, knees tucked to my chest, letting the chill of the tile seep through my clothes. Breathe, Savvy.

The door rattled.

"Open up, it's us." Ivy's voice carried that edge she reserved for wedding-day meltdowns and mascara emergencies.

My hands shook as I lifted and flipped the lock. Ivy burst in first, a whirlwind of honey-blonde hair and concern, with Maddy behind her, pulling emergency tissues from her bag.

"What happened?" Maddy's question carried the weight of five years of avoided conversations.

"Henry." His name made my throat close. "My mark was Henry."

"Seriously, Savvy," Maddy said. "Henry ... as in—"

"As in, why I'm hiding in a bathroom instead of finishing a job? Yes." I slid back down to the floor, my legs refusing to hold me up any longer. "Caroline hired me to break up with him."

"Caroline who?" Maddy sat beside me, her shoulder pressed against mine. The familiar scent of her shampoo—the same Japanese cherry blossom she'd used since high school—wrapped around me like a security blanket.

"His girlfriend. Well, almost fiancée." I laughed, the sound closer to a sob. "He had a ring."

"Oh, honey." Ivy crouched in front of me, her face a mirror of that night five years ago when she'd found me crying on the bookstore floor. She'd stayed with me until sunrise. Then, we both curled up in the window seat while I waited for texts that never came.

"Tell us everything." Maddy's arm slid around my shoulders, pulling me closer. We'd perfected this formation years ago—me in the middle, Maddy solid and steady on one side, Ivy fierce and protective on the other. Through first heartbreaks and college finals, failed business plans and rebuilt dreams, this was our default setting. We were an unbreakable trio.

"I walked in, and he was … there." The words tumbled out between shaky breaths. "Sitting at my usual table, looking exactly the same but completely different."

"Different, how?" Ivy's hand found mine, her fingers cool against my palm.

"Sadder? Tired?" I closed my eyes, but his face was still there. "God, I actually picked up his ring from the floor. Who does that? Who picks up their ex's engagement ring for someone else?"

"Someone who's built a career out of giving others the closure she never got." Maddy's words hit hard. She'd been the one to say the hard truths we needed to hear.

"You know what the worst part is?" My voice cracked, barely above a whisper. "He looked relieved. He didn't seem surprised when I told him his girlfriend wanted to break up. Just … relieved."

"Like he'd been looking for a way out?" Ivy's thumb traced circles on my hand like she'd done during thunderstorms when we were kids.

"Like someone had unlocked his cage, and he was free to fly." I leaned my head against the wall, the pressure of it all settling over me. "It's not that he didn't want to marry her. It's that he can't seem to love anyone. Not her. Not me. I spent so much time wondering if I ever meant anything to him, and I think I have my answer. He's not capable of loving anyone."

"Hey." Maddy's voice adopted that calm she used when we started spiraling. "You don't know what's going on in his life. Remember what we promised after that night?"

"No more writing other people's stories for them." Ivy and I echoed the familiar mantra.

"Exactly." Maddy squeezed my shoulder. "So, stop trying to write his."

A knock on the door made us all jump. "Everything okay in there. You've been in there for over an hour?" the Paper Crane's owner called out. "Do I need to call someone?"

"We're good, Mrs. Clark!" Ivy called back. "Just a minor crisis of the heart."

"Ah." The understanding in her voice spoke volumes. "Take your time. I'll put on some tea."

"I'm fine, no time for tea." I smoothed my blazer again, a nervous tell I thought I'd eliminated years ago. "I have two more clients today. I can do this."

"Like hell you are." Maddy's voice sharpened. "You sent us a 911 text."

"You can't seriously be thinking about going back out there," Ivy added. "Not after—"

"I needed to make sure." My voice cracked on the words. "That you'd still..."

"Hey." Ivy's arms wrapped around me. "We're not going anywhere. Ever."

"Not like him." Maddy joined our huddle, her chin resting on my shoulder. "You're stuck with us, Sav."

I breathed in their familiar scents, finding reassurance in their presence. "Cork & Crown after my last client?"

"Obviously. Who says we have to limit our wine nights to Wednesdays anyway?" Ivy squeezed my hand. "Some emergencies require throwing out the rule book."

I nodded. "Five o'clock?"

"We'll be there." Maddy opened the bathroom door. "Try not to break anyone too badly before then."

But as I walked out of The Paper Crane, my heels striking the pavement in a steady rhythm, all I could think about was how Henry's hands had shaken when he'd reached for his coffee cup—the relief in his eyes when I'd delivered Caroline's goodbye.

LE PAIN QUOTIDIEN was wedged between a vintage record store and an artisanal cheese shop, every inch of it calculated to appeal to tech entrepreneurs who thought five-dollar croissants made them cosmopolitan. Usually, I appreciated its predictability—the rustic wooden tables, the overpriced lattes, the constant hum of laptops and self-importance.

Today, everything was off-kilter. I claimed my usual corner table, but instead of feeling like command central, it seemed exposed. Vulnerable. The curated playlist that normally faded into background noise seemed to mock me with its endless parade of love songs.

My mark arrived right on schedule—a startup CEO fresh from his latest round of venture capital funding. His Patagonia vest and perfectly trimmed stubble screamed Silicon Valley wannabe. Normally, I'd be cataloging his tells, planning my approach. Instead, I could only think about how Henry's coffee cup rattled against its saucer.

"Jennifer?" He extended his hand. "Thanks for meeting with me. I've got some exciting projections to show you."

It's the same opening line. The same practiced smile. How many times had I done this? How often had I sat across from someone who thought they were heading for a business meeting, only to deliver someone else's goodbye?

I forced my voice steady. "When your girlfriend asked me to meet with you—"

"Tabitha reached out to you?" His face lit up. "That's

great! We've been talking about expanding her wellness brand into—"

"She feels that your relationship has run its course." The words sat heavy on my tongue, bitter and sharp like unripe fruit. How many courses had life run? How many times had someone else decided your path for you?

His expression stiffened. "What?"

"She says you never let her in." Just like Henry had kept me locked out of the parts of himself that mattered most. *No. Focus.* This wasn't about Henry. "She's tired of feeling like a stranger in her own relationship."

"But ... but we signed a lease together."

"She'll be out by the end of the week." My voice was steady, professional—the foundation of my reputation. "She thinks it's for the best. A clean break. No messy endings."

He let out a sharp, bitter laugh. "No messy endings? She didn't even have the guts to tell me herself!"

Like someone else I knew. Someone who vanished without a word. Five years had passed, and I still didn't know what I'd done wrong.

Stop it. This isn't about you.

"Sometimes distance brings clarity." The words felt hollow. How many times had I repeated them? How often had I tried to believe them?

His voice cracked. "Distance? We had dinner plans tonight. We were talking about getting a dog."

Just like Henry and I had talked about forever. Like we'd planned our future over coffee and dreams and promises worth less than the paper napkins we'd written them on.

Focus, Savvy.

But my carefully constructed script rang empty for the

first time in three years. Every word, every practiced gesture, betrayed something I couldn't quite define.

I reached for my portfolio, needing something solid to hold on to. "She wanted you to know—"

"No." He stood abruptly, his chair scraping against the floor. "I don't want to hear what she wanted me to know. I want to hear it from her."

My throat closed. I'd wished for that same chance more times than I could count. I'd replayed that last conversation with Henry over and over, wondering what signs I'd missed.

"Sometimes," I heard myself say, the words coming from some deep, broken place I thought I'd buried, "we don't get the endings we deserve."

He stared at me for a long moment, seeing something in my face that made his anger fade to something softer, sadder. "Sounds like you know that from experience."

I stood, straightening my blazer. Professional distance. Always professional distance. "Your lease termination papers will arrive tomorrow. She's already signed them."

But as I walked out into the October sunshine, my next client's details pulled up on my phone, an unsettled feeling curled in my chest. Something fundamental had changed. Like the ground beneath my world had developed hairline cracks, threatening to shatter everything I'd built on top of it.

One more client. I could do one more.

I had to.

Because if I stopped now—if I let myself dwell too long on Henry's unsteady hands and eyes brimming with relief, on rings that seemed flawless but didn't feel right, on all the endings that never got their proper goodbyes—I might never find the courage to do this again.

Rise and Grind Coffee loomed ahead like a bad joke. Of

course, my last client would be here. The universe wasn't done torturing me yet.

I paused outside, my reflection ghostly in the window: same blue blazer, same professional mask, same armor. But the woman staring back at me looked like she'd aged five years in five hours.

"You came back." Marcus didn't bother hiding his surprise as I walked in. "After this morning, I thought—"

"Don't," I said. "Just ... pretend this morning never happened."

His eyes warmed with understanding. "Your usual table is open."

I claimed my spot, muscle memory guiding me as I arranged my portfolio, phone, and defenses. But Henry's presence clung to the air like a trace of perfume—the way his voice had cracked on my name, the tremor in his hands, the relief in his eyes that struck like a fresh betrayal.

Focus. Client 345. Investment banker, recently made partner. A girlfriend of three years thinks his success means he gets to plan everyone else's life.

The bell chimed. Right on time—polished shoes, tailored suit, Rolex catching the light. Everything about him screamed success and security.

Everything that Henry's ring had promised Caroline.
Stop it.

"Jennifer?" He extended his hand, gold cufflinks glinting. "Charles Matthews. Thanks for meeting with me. I've got some promising opportunities to discuss."

I gestured to the chair across from me, the one Henry had occupied hours earlier. "When your girlfriend asked me to meet with you—"

"Sarah?" His expression turned almost patronizing. "She's ready to discuss a proper business plan? I've told her she needs to think bigger than that little yoga studio. It's charming, sure, but it's not exactly a legacy."

The familiar script rose to my lips, but something else came out instead. "When was the last time you took a class there?"

He blinked, thrown off script. "I'm sorry?"

"Her yoga studio. You called it 'little.'" Like Henry's father had called the marina quaint. "But have you seen how she lights up when discussing it? How many lives she's changing?"

"I ... I don't see what this has to do with—"

"She's leaving you." The words came out sharper than my usual delivery. "Because while you've been planning her empire, you missed what she's built. A community. Not a corporation."

Color rose in his cheeks. "Now, wait a minute—"

"She tried to tell you. Every time you turned her dreams into a business plan. Every time you treated her passion like it needed fixing." My hands were clenched under the table. "Every time you confused money with meaning."

Oh god. This wasn't about Sarah and Charles anymore. This wasn't even close to professional.

Charles's face hardened into the mask I usually wore. "I've given her everything."

"Except a choice." The words burned my throat. "You decided what she needed, what was best for her future. Did you ever think maybe she wanted to make those decisions herself?"

He leaned back, studying me with narrowed eyes. "This isn't really about Sarah, is it?"

The question hit me hard. Professional distance crumbled like wet paper. After years of perfectly scripted good-byes, I sat here projecting my hurt onto a stranger's story.

"I apologize." I straightened my portfolio. "That was unprofessional. Your girlfriend asked me to inform you she's ending your relationship. She'll be moved out by Monday."

"Just like that?" His voice carried an edge of desperation I recognized too well. "Three years, and she sends a stranger to end it?"

It's like five years and not even a goodbye.

"Sometimes—" My voice cracked. I cleared my throat and tried again. "Sometimes people make choices for us. All we can do is live with them."

"Or fight back." He stood, pushing his chair in with precise movements. "I'm not letting her go without an explanation. Not like this."

Something painful lodged in my chest. Fight back. Had I fought back? Had I done anything except build a career around other people's endings?

He turned back briefly at the door, his expression hard but determined. "Some things are worth fighting for."

I watched him go, his words echoing in my head. *Were they true?* Or was it another pretty lie we told ourselves when the truth hurt too much?

Marcus appeared at my elbow with a cup of tea I hadn't ordered. "On the house." He hesitated. "That's the first time I've seen you lose your script."

"That obvious?"

"Only to someone who's watched you break hearts professionally for years." He set down a chocolate croissant next to the tea. "Also, no charge. You look like you need it."

I stared at my reflection on the tea's surface. The perfect professional mask had cracked, showing glimpses of the girl who'd once believed in forever—the girl who'd trusted a pair of blue eyes and promises written on coffee shop napkins.

My phone buzzed.

MADDY

Are you on your way? Wine and chocolate will be waiting.

IVY

And shoulders to cry on if needed.

I gathered my things, tucking away the remnants of my professional persona. Two failed meetings. Two breaks from the script. Two cracks in the foundation of everything I'd built.

"Thanks, Marcus." I stood, legs steadier than I deserved. "For everything."

"You know," he called after me, "some things are supposed to break. Makes room for something stronger to grow."

I pushed through the door into the late afternoon sunshine, his words tangling with Charles's in my mind. Some things matter more than clean breaks. Some things are supposed to break.

As I boarded the train to River Bend and headed for Cork & Crown, I wondered—maybe some things weren't meant to break. Maybe they were meant to bend, to change, to grow.

Maybe it was time to find out.

CORK & Crown's familiar warmth wrapped around me when I pushed through the door. Gloria looked up from polishing wine glasses, her usual smile fading as she took in my face.

"Oh, sweetie." She reached for a bottle without asking. "That bad?"

"Henry bad." My voice cracked on his name.

Her hands stilled on the wineglass. "Our Henry?"

As if there could be another. As if anyone else could shatter my professional persona so thoroughly. I sank onto my usual stool, dropping my head into my hands. "He was my mark today."

"Well, shit." The curse sounded foreign in Gloria's elegant voice, like a diamond slipped into a pile of gravel. She set a glass before me, the deep red liquid catching the early evening light. "Where are my daughter and Ivy?"

"Here!" Maddy burst through the door with Ivy right behind her.

"You look worse than you did this morning," Ivy said, sliding onto the stool beside me.

"That's because this morning, I only had to deal with Henry." I took a long sip of wine, savoring the warmth as it spread through my chest. "This afternoon, I had to be professional."

"How'd that go?" Maddy asked, hopping onto the stool on my other side, her eyes brimming with curiosity.

"I may have been projecting my unresolved Henry baggage onto other people's breakups."

Gloria snorted. "May have?"

"Okay, fine. I definitely did." I stared into my wineglass, the liquid catching the light like a mirror I didn't want to look into. "It's a problem."

"You think?" Ivy raised an eyebrow but eased it with a teasing grin. "Do we need to stage an intervention?"

"No intervention necessary," I muttered. "Just ... a reminder to keep my personal baggage out of my professional life. Clearly, I need it."

Gloria shook her head, half-laughing. "Well, at least you're self-aware. That's step one, right?"

"On a scale of one to the dove incident," Maddy said. "How bad did it go?"

"I sabotaged my reputation." I took another long sip. "Years of perfect composure, ruined because Henry Kingston got engaged in my territory."

"Almost engaged," Ivy corrected, signaling Gloria for another round. "And technically, you did your job. Caroline's message was delivered."

"Along with some bonus commentary." I swirled the wine in my glass, the buzz hitting faster than usual—probably because I'd skipped lunch, opting instead to hide in a bathroom and question my life choices.

Gloria set fresh glasses before us, then pulled out a bottle I recognized as her special reserve. "If any day deserves the good stuff, it's this one."

"Mom." Maddy's eyes widened. "That's your birthday wine."

"And my only daughter's best friend had to deliver someone else's breakup to the love of her life." Gloria's voice carried that mom's tone, which broke down all defenses. "I think that qualifies as an event."

"He wasn't—" The lie died on my lips as the wine loosened my tongue. "God, who am I kidding? Of course, he was. Still is, probably. How pathetic is that?"

"Not pathetic." Ivy squeezed my hand. "Human."

"You know what's pathetic?" The words spilled out faster now, helped by Gloria's expensive wine. "I kept the napkin. The one where he drew out our future. Little house by the river, room for a garden, space for my books." I laughed, and the sound edged with hysteria. "I built my entire business doing the opposite of everything we planned, and I still kept that stupid napkin."

"Honey." Gloria reached across the bar, her hand cool

against my flushed cheek. "That's not pathetic. That's hope."

"Hope is dangerous." But even as I said it, I could feel my walls crumbling. "Hope makes you keep a napkin for five years. Hope makes you wonder if there was a good reason why the guy you loved disappeared." The room swam as I reached for my glass. "Hope makes you look into his eyes today and still see everything you lost."

Maddy and Ivy exchanged a look over my head. The same look they'd given each other the night Henry disappeared when they'd found me in the bookstore.

"Maybe," Maddy said, "hope keeps us human."

"Then I don't want to be human anymore." The words came out slurred. "I want to be professional. Untouchable. Not this ... mess who just told a client his girlfriend was right to leave him."

"You're not a mess." Ivy's arm slid around my shoulders. "You're feeling things. Finally."

"I don't want to feel things." But the tears came anyway, hot and fast. "I don't want to wonder why he looked relieved when I delivered Caroline's goodbye. I don't want to think about that ring; it's so perfect and wrong. I don't want to remember how his hands shook, the way he takes his coffee, or how he smells like..." I hiccuped. "Like home."

"Okay." Gloria started putting away wine glasses with purpose. "That's enough public emotional processing for one evening. Maddy, Ivy—make sure she gets home okay."

"On it," Maddy said, slipping an arm around my waist.

Ivy flanked my other side. "We've got you, Sav."

The cool night air hit my face as we stepped outside, the short walk to the bookstore stretching endlessly before me. Maddy and Ivy kept me steady, their quiet presence a lifeline as Main Street swam in and out of focus.

"Almost there," Ivy murmured as we approached the familiar storefront, the 'Closed' sign glowing softly in the window.

They each grabbed an arm to help me up the stairs to my apartment above the shop, but I stopped shy of the door. "Okay, thanks, but I've got it from here."

Maddy narrowed her eyes at me. "No way. We're coming in."

"I appreciate it, but I'm fine," I insisted, tugging my arm free from Ivy's grip. "I need to face plant into bed, and you two don't need to babysit me for that."

"You can barely walk straight," Ivy countered, her voice sharp with worry.

"And yet, I can still walk. Trust me, I'll text when I'm in bed. Go home."

They exchanged glances—one of those silent best-friend arguments that don't need words—before Maddy huffed, "Fine. But you *better* text."

"I promise," I said, fumbling for my keys.

"Goodnight, then," Ivy said reluctantly as they backed down the stairs, still watching me like I might topple over at any second. "Call if you need anything. And I mean anything."

I nodded, watching as they disappeared down the stairs and into the night, their voices fading as they walked back up Main Street. Leaning heavily against my door, I tried again to fit the key into the lock, the ghost of Henry's relief-filled eyes haunting me.

CHAPTER SEVEN

Henry

I shouldn't be here. That's all I could think as I watched Savvy struggle with her keys, the glow from River Bend Books' window casting shadows across her face. All those years of wondering, regretting, and telling myself it was for the best. And now, I was hiding in the darkness like a stalker.

She'd been unsteady on her feet the moment Maddy and Ivy had disappeared around the corner, their laughter still echoing up the street. Part of me wondered if I should leave, pretend I hadn't seen how she'd swayed against the door, the fumbling dance of her hands as she tried to fit the key into the lock.

But then she stumbled, pitching backward with a startled cry, and I was moving before I could second-guess myself. I took the stairs two at a time, catching her before she hit the ground.

"Got you." The words scraped raw in my throat as her

body curved into mine, fitting against me like the missing piece of a puzzle I'd been trying to forget. My arms tightened instinctively around her waist, muscle memory making fools of us both.

She melted against me for a heartbeat—one perfect, terrible moment where time seemed to stop—before going rigid. "No." Her palm pressed against my chest, and I knew she could feel my heart racing beneath her fingers like it always had at her touch. "Can't be you. Universe isn't that cruel."

"Pretty sure it is." I repositioned her, cradling her against me like something precious and dangerous. One arm beneath her shoulders, the other under her knees—the same way I'd carried her through summer storms and across dew-damp grass, over thresholds we'd dreamed about but never crossed. Her head found the hollow of my throat as if she'd never forgotten the way she fit there, and the familiar feel made my chest ache with everything we'd lost.

"Put me down." Her voice wavered, but the way her fingers curled into my shirt betrayed her. Her head tilted against me like some of her still remembered this and *us*.

"I hate you," she whispered, her voice unsteady with defiance—contradicted by the way she stayed close. "I hate that being near you still feels like home."

That hit like a gut punch. *Home.* Wasn't that what I'd wanted to be for her? The thing I hadn't been brave enough to fight for?

"You're bleeding." A thin line of blood trickled down her leg where she'd scraped it against the railing.

"Don't care." She jabbed a finger at my chest. "Why are you here? Are you stalking me? Because that's..." She swayed in my arms, frowning as she searched for the word.

"That's bad. Terrible." She sighed, her shoulders sagging. "I wished bad things on you. Like warts. Or a third arm."

"No warts. No third arms," I said, retrieving her keys from where they'd fallen. "Let's get you inside before you hurt yourself worse."

Getting her door open while holding her proved challenging, especially with her alternating between going completely boneless in my arms and suddenly trying to escape. Adjusting my grip, I nudged the door open with my shoulder and stepped inside.

As I crossed into her apartment, it hit me—this was Savvy's space, her life after me, and every detail was like a clue I wasn't sure I wanted to decipher.

I adjusted her, her head falling against my shoulder, and entered the living room. A worn leather couch sat across from a wall of mismatched frames. Colorful throw pillows were scattered haphazardly like she'd tossed them there in a hurry. A large bookshelf dominated one wall, crammed with titles ranging from classic literature to modern thrillers. I recognized a few of her favorites from college. Their spines were creased, and covers faded from countless re-reads.

But the photos were what caught my eye.

Still holding her, I moved closer to the frames on the shelf. Snapshots of a life I hadn't been part of stared back at me—Savvy and her parents at her college graduation, their faces alight with pride and emotions too big for words. Then there was Savvy, Maddy, and Ivy, dressed in Halloween costumes: Savvy as a mischievous pirate with a crooked hat and plastic sword, Maddy as a glitter-covered fairy with wings askew, and Ivy as a zombie bride, veil trailing as they laughed at some unheard joke.

I tore my gaze away, my arms aching from holding her.

"Where's your first aid kit?" I asked, my voice strained but steady.

"Not telling." She crossed her arms—or at least tried to—before grabbing my shirt to steady herself. "Because you're not the one who gets to care for me anymore. You lost that right somewhere between 'forever' and 'ghost mode activated.'"

Christ. Drunk Savvy had always been honest, but this was like taking a razor blade straight to the jugular. "Come on, Savvy. Let me get a Band-Aid."

"Bathroom," she sighed as if conceding some small battle. "Under the sink. Not because I'm helping you. I just ... don't want to bleed on my new rug. Mom would kill me."

Navigating her unfamiliar space, I carried her down the hall, every step feeling like an intrusion. The bathroom door was ajar, light spilling into the hallway. I shifted her gently, setting her on the counter, her legs dangling over the edge as she blinked up at me, unfocused.

"This is weird," she murmured as I wet a washcloth. "You're being weird. Why are you being weird in my bathroom? And why is my bathroom spinning?"

"Because you probably drank your weight in wine," I replied, keeping my voice light as emotions churned.

"No," she muttered, clutching the counter's edge for balance. "Because you're Henry. My Henry. No, wait. Not my Henry. Just ... Henry."

Her fingers brushed my collar as I dabbed the scrape with a damp washcloth. She winced, her knee twitching like she wasn't sure whether to pull away or hold still.

"That hurts."

"It's water, Savvy," I said, steadying my voice.

"Well, it doesn't *feel* like water; it's like fire," she shot back, slumping against the mirror with a dramatic huff.

"You're impossible."

"I am *not* impossible," she argued, dragging out the word like it was my fault. "You're heavy-handed. Like a caveman. A caveman with stupid, nice hands..."

Her voice faltered, and her brow furrowed as if she had realized what she said. I focused on securing the bandage, ignoring the way a knot formed in my chest.

"Let's get you to bed," I said.

Her bedroom was down the hall, the door ajar. I nudged it open with my foot, moonlight spilling across a space that was unmistakably Savvy—books on nearly every surface, a reading nook under the window, and fairy lights glowing faintly above the bed.

"You still make terrible life choices," she mumbled as I set her gently on the mattress. "Like showing up here. Like still smelling like you did back then. Like making me remember ... when I don't want to."

"Sleep, Savvy." I pulled the quilt over her, my hand lingering for a moment on her shoulder.

"You can't tell me what to do anymore," she whispered, curling onto her side, hair spilling across the pillow. "You lost that right when you decided I wasn't worth your time."

The words hit like a physical blow. I stayed there for a beat, watching her breathing slowly, her expression relaxing in sleep.

"You were worth everything," I murmured, the confession slipping out. But she was gone to the world, leaving me alone in the silence.

I stood by her bed a moment longer, exhaling slowly. "You always did make a place feel like home." It was a space entirely *hers*, familiar and foreign, like seeing the outline of someone you used to know.

We needed to talk. There was too much between us now, too much unsaid. And if there was any chance to fix the broken pieces, it would have to start somewhere.

Careful not to wake her, I left the room. In the kitchen, I grabbed a glass and filled it with water, then dug through drawers until I found a bottle of aspirin. I brought them back, setting the glass and the pills gently on her nightstand. She stirred, but her breathing remained steady.

I watched her for another moment. This was Savvy—*my* Savvy—and yet not mine at all. She'd built a life I'd never been part of, and every inch of this apartment reminded me of that. But it also brought back what we'd once been. We were mornings at Common Grounds spent laughing over coffee, promises that seemed unshakable.

I spotted a notepad on her desk, its corner sticking out from under a stack of books. After a moment's hesitation, I grabbed it and a black Sharpie.

When I glanced back at her, she turned over, and her bandaged knee slipped into view, catching the light. I couldn't help myself. A weight settled in my chest as I stared, then I forced myself to move.

I left the Sharpie on the desk, staring at the note one last time before sliding it under the water glass. Exhaling slowly, I told myself it wasn't just a note but a peace offering.

I left the apartment, locked the door behind me, and stepped into the cool night air. It was sharp against my skin, but it did nothing to ease the ache in my chest. Seeing Savvy like this, getting a glimpse into the life she'd built without me, was a poignant reminder of everything I'd given up. And everything I'd taken from her.

I slid into the driver's seat of my car and gripped the

steering wheel until the strain ached up my arms. All those years of telling myself I'd done the right thing, that walking away had been the only way to protect her—now, I wasn't so sure.

With the image of her tears burned into my mind, I couldn't quiet the voice whispering that maybe I'd been wrong all along.

CHAPTER EIGHT

Savvy

Morning attacked with the subtlety of a sledgehammer, sunlight streaming through curtains I'd forgotten to close. My head throbbed in time with my pulse. Each beat was a reminder that wine was not, in fact, a solution to my Henry Kingston problem.

Fragments of yesterday filtered through the hangover haze. Crying in The Paper Crane's bathroom. Gloria's special reserve wine. Almost falling down the stairs and—

No.

My eyes snapped open, then immediately slammed shut against the brutal morning light. That part had to be a dream—his powerful arms catching me, his voice saying my name like a prayer and a curse wrapped into one word.

Henry Kingston had not carried me into my home after Maddy and Ivy left. That was my drunk brain creating the worst possible scenario to torture me with. Next, my imagination would try to convince me I'd told him he smelled the same, or worse, that I'd—

"Oh god." I pressed my face into my pillow, memories flooding back with mortifying clarity. I had told him he smelled the same. And then I'd said ... no, I couldn't even finish the thought without wanting to die of embarrassment.

Pushing myself up on shaky arms, I winced at the throb in my knee. Looking down, I found a perfectly applied bandage with a tiny smiley face drawn in the corner. My stomach dropped.

Only one person had ever done that—a ridiculous habit he'd started the summer I kept scraping my knees helping Dad repair boats at the marina. "A happy bandage heals faster," he'd say, adding his signature smile with a black Sharpie.

No. No, no, no.

Two aspirin and a glass of water waited on my nightstand, and something crinkled underneath—a note written in that familiar, precise handwriting that still appeared in my dreams.

Common Grounds. 9 a.m.

I forced myself upright, fumbling for the aspirin. After swallowing the pills with a sip of water, I dragged myself to the bathroom. As the shower heated, I brushed my teeth, then stepped under the spray for a quick rinse. The moment I stepped out, my phone buzzed.

MADDY

You alive? You didn't text.

IVY

Did you make it to bed okay? We probably shouldn't have left you alone.

ME

I'm fine. Just hungover.

I stared at my reflection in the steamy mirror, debating whether to tell them about Henry's appearance. They'd dropped everything to rescue me at The Paper Crane yesterday. They'd been there for the original heartbreak, holding, supporting, and loving me. If anyone would understand how quickly my walls had crumbled, it would be them.

But telling them meant admitting that one touch had turned me back into that girl who believed in forever. That girl they'd worked so hard to help me bury.

I took another look at the smiley face on my bandage. They deserved to know.

ME

Something happened after you left last night.

MADDY

What do you mean?

Taking a deep breath, I typed the words that would change everything.

ME

Henry showed up.

IVY

WHAT?

MADDY

Henry KINGSTON?

ME

No, Henry the VIII. YES, HENRY KINGSTON!

IVY

Details. Now.

MADDY

Why didn't you call us?

The story spilled out in a series of texts—how I'd almost fallen, how he'd caught me, carried me into my home. With each message, I waited for their judgment, their anger at my weakness.

IVY

Maybe this is your chance.

ME

My chance for what? More humiliation?

MADDY

Your chance for closure. Real closure is not the kind you give other people.

ME

I don't need closure. I need professional distance.

IVY

Honey, you were never getting professional distance from Henry Kingston.

MADDY

Maybe it's time to take your own advice. Clean breaks, remember?

ME

This feels more like reopening an old wound.

IVY

Or maybe healing it properly this time.

I stared at his note again, the precise strokes of his handwriting as familiar as my own. Common Grounds. A place that had seen so many beginnings and endings, including ours.

ME

He left a note. Wants to meet at 9.

MADDY

Are you going?

ME

Of course not. I have clients.

IVY

Is that true, or are you hiding?

ME

Since when have you questioned my schedule?

MADDY

Since you had an emotional breakdown about him yesterday.

ME

I'm not going.

But I was pulling on my most comfortable jeans and a blazer because, apparently, years of meticulously built walls meant nothing in the face of Henry Kingston's desire to talk.

THE OCTOBER MORNING hit me like a slap as I stepped outside, the crisp autumn air doing nothing to clear my head. River Bend was awake and bustling. Mrs. Patterson was power walking past with her tiny dog, Mr. Dixon was arranging the same never-sold antiques in The

Weathered Barn's display, and Mom was organizing the weekly "Staff Picks" in the front of River Bend Books.

I tried to slip past the store without being seen, but Mom's radar for emotional distress was legendary.

"Savannah Rose Honeysucker," she called from the door. Her voice had that edge that meant she was fully aware of the mess I'd gotten myself into. "Going somewhere?"

"A client meeting." The lie was heavy on my tongue.

She emerged with her reading glasses perched on her head. "In baggy jeans?"

I looked down at my outfit. "I'm trying a fresh approach?"

"Mm-hmm." She studied my face with that mom-intensity that made me feel about five years old. "Would this approach have anything to do with why Henry Kingston's car was parked in the alley behind the bookstore last night?"

My heart stopped. "You saw him?"

"Honey, everyone saw him. It's River Bend. Mrs. Patterson's updated her neighborhood watch group chat twice."

Perfect. Just perfect.

"It's not—" I started, then stopped because I had no idea what it wasn't. "I have to go."

"Savvy." She caught my arm as I tried to escape. "Whatever you're running toward—or from—remember something."

"That Henry Kingston broke my heart and turned me into someone who breaks hearts professionally?"

"No, that you're braver now than you were then." She squeezed my arm. "And courage isn't just about putting up defenses. Sometimes, it's about knowing which ones to take down."

"Mom—"

"Go," she said. "But maybe stop by Timeless Treats first. Karen's got your blueberry muffin waiting."

"How did—"

"Mrs. Patterson's group chat is very thorough. Henry was seen buying two coffees ten minutes ago at Common Grounds."

Of course, he was. Because Henry Kingston did nothing halfway—not breaking hearts, not disappearing from my life, and not whatever this was.

The path to Common Grounds hadn't changed in five years. It's the same worn dirt track, the same gnarly oak roots trying to trip unwary hikers, the same glimpses of the Hudson through autumn leaves. But everything else was different. The girl who used to run up this path, eager to meet Henry for sunrise coffee at our favorite coffee shop, was gone. In her place was someone tougher, someone who'd learned that forever was just another pretty lie people told themselves.

I heard him before I saw him—the soft hum he likely didn't even realize he was making. My feet stopped moving of their own accord, my heart pounding against my ribs. There he was, seated in our old spot atop the hilltop café, two coffee cups beside him, gazing out over the Hudson River as if the past had never happened.

The morning sunlight caught his profile, highlighting the changes time had carved into him. His jaw was sharper, a premature touch of silver threading through his dark hair at the temples. The boy who'd promised me forever had grown into a man who looked every inch the Kingston heir —except for how his fingers drummed against his coffee cup, a nervous tell I remembered too well.

"You came." Five years of unspoken words echoed in his voice.

My fingers curled into fists. "You can't leave notes and expect me to show up."

He fixed his gaze on the river, his jawline sharp in the morning light. "But you did."

The space between us hummed with everything left unsaid—endings we never wanted and beginnings we never had. "You ambushed me."

"Seems fitting." Now he turned, and the morning light caught his handsome face—dark hair tousled just right, piercing blue eyes that held a familiar intensity, and the perfect amount of scruff that made my inner thighs tingle. "Since you did the same to me yesterday at Rise and Grind."

"That wasn't—" I crossed my arms. "I didn't know it was you."

"I know." He held out one of the coffee cups. "Peace offering?"

The rich scent of perfectly-made coffee drifted between us, another memory he'd weaponized without trying.

"Peace isn't my business model anymore."

"No." Something stirred in his eyes. "Breaking hearts is more your style now."

"Does that seem familiar?" The words came out sharper than I intended. "You wrote the manual."

He winced. Actually winced. "I deserve that."

"You deserve a lot of things." I took the coffee. "Most which involve bodily harm."

"I remember." He patted the seat beside him. "You always did have creative ideas about revenge."

"Don't." I stayed standing, the coffee burning hot against my palms. "Don't do that thing where you pretend we're still those people. Where you act like you didn't ... vanish."

"Savvy—"

"No." My fingers tightened around the coffee cup. "You can't just 'Savvy' me with that voice. Not after years of silence. Not after I had to find out about your engagement in a client meeting."

"Almost engagement." He set his coffee down. "Though you ended that pretty thoroughly."

"I was doing my job."

"And what is that?"

"Delivering the truth." I took a sip to stop myself from saying more, then nearly choked. Perfect. He remembered exactly how I liked it. "Why are you here, Henry?"

"Because I owe you an explanation."

"You owed me an explanation five years ago." Another sip of coffee, another stab of memory. How many mornings had we spent here, planning futures that never happened? "Now, you owe me professional courtesy. You can contact me through my business if you want to speak to me. The Breakup Broker. Caroline has the number."

"That's ... that's really what you're doing now?" He laughed, but there was no humor in it. "Breaking up with people for money?"

"As opposed to what? Calling it quits through total silence and ghosting? At least I give people closure."

"Is that what you tell yourself?" he asked, subtly leaning forward to close the distance between us, his fingers lightly tapping the table. "That you're providing a service? That it's better your way?"

"It is better," I replied, my voice shaking and betraying the lie. "Clean breaks. No messy endings. No waiting for texts that never come or explanations that never arrive."

"Savvy..."

"Don't." I stepped back, creating space between us.

"You have no right to psychoanalyze my career choices. Not when you're the reason they exist."

"I know." He ran a hand through his hair—a gesture so familiar it hurt. "God, Savvy, I know. That's why I'm here. To explain—"

"I don't want your explanation." But even as I said it, I knew it was a lie. "I want nothing from you except distance. Just stay in your world, and I'll stay in mine."

"That's not possible anymore."

"Why? Because you found out what I do for a living? Because your girlfriend hired me to dump you?" I forced a laugh. "Don't worry. I'll refund her fee as a professional courtesy. It didn't go down the way it should have."

"No, because my grandfather asked to see you."

"Your grandfather?" I blinked, sure I'd misheard. "Why would James want to see me?"

Henry's jaw tightened. "Because he's dying."

The words hung between us, heavy with a history I'd tried so hard to forget. James Morrison was the only person in Henry's family who saw me.

"I'm sorry." The words were hollow, inadequate. "I had no idea he was sick."

"He doesn't want people to know." Henry looked down at his coffee cup. "He wants to go out on his own terms, like always."

"Sounds like James." I swallowed past the lump in my throat. "But I still don't understand. Why me? Why now?"

"Please, Savvy." His voice carried an urgency I'd never heard before. "He doesn't have much time left. And this ... this is important to him. He's at Madison Center."

I watched the sun glinting off the Hudson, remembering all the times James had defended me to his son, how he'd slipped me books he thought I'd enjoy, complete with handwritten notes about why each story reminded him of me.

"Fine." I set my coffee down, needing my hands free to maintain my composure. "I'll see James. But that's it. One visit, one conversation, and then we return to our separate worlds."

Relief flashed across his face, followed by something harder to read. "Thank you. I'll pick you up at five."

"I'm not doing it for you." I gathered my coffee and bag, every movement measured and controlled. "I'm doing it for the only Kingston who ever thought I belonged in your world. Don't bother picking me up. I'll take the train."

I walked away. Behind me, the river flowed like it had for five years without Henry Kingston. The same way it would keep flowing long after this moment.

My phone buzzed as I reached the bottom of the path.

MADDY
Well?

ME
His grandfather wants to see me.

IVY
James? The only good one in the family?

ME
The same.

MADDY
Are you going?

I stared at the question for a long moment, remembering James's kind eyes and quiet wisdom.

ME
Yes. But not for Henry.

IVY

Remember—you're not that girl anymore.

MADDY

No. You're the woman who built a career out of other people's endings. Don't let him make you forget that.

I caught my reflection in a store window. They were right—I wasn't that starry-eyed college girl anymore. So why did one coffee with Henry Kingston make me feel like she was beneath the surface, waiting to believe in forever again?

But as I headed home to change, I couldn't remove the memory of his voice saying my name.

Damn Henry Kingston and his perfect coffee memory. And damn that stupid smiley face still grinning up at me from my bandage.

CHAPTER NINE

Henry

I watched Savvy disappear down the trail, her words still echoing in my ears. "I'm not doing it for you."

The hurt in her eyes had cut deeper than any of the sharp words she'd hurled at me. I deserved them—every last one. I deserved worse for what I'd done to her.

Taking a shaky breath, I sipped the lukewarm coffee in my hand, its harsh tang doing nothing to ease the ache in my chest. Part of me had foolishly hoped that seeing her again after all these years wouldn't hurt so much. Maybe enough time had passed for the guilt to fade, replaced by something softer—nostalgia.

But seeing her this morning hit me like a tidal wave. The years had done nothing to dull the impact. Every barrier I'd built around my heart shattered, leaving me raw and exposed in a way I hadn't been since the day I walked away.

I drained the last of my coffee and stood, my body moving on autopilot as I headed back to the car. My grandfather's request had brought me here, but the burden of it pressed harder with every step. I never should have asked Savvy to come see him—not after everything I'd put her through.

What right did I have to drag her into my family's mess? To reopen old wounds? To force her to face the man who'd fled without a fight?

Sliding into the driver's seat, I gripped the steering wheel tightly, the ache in my chest refusing to ease. The streets of River Bend stretched before me, quiet and familiar, yet hollow without her. Once, being here—being with her—made me feel like I belonged. Like I'd found something solid to hold on to.

Everything was different. The town remained the same —I was the one who had changed. And without Savvy, the sense of belonging I once clung to was gone, replaced by a hollow ache that refused to be ignored.

I started the car, the engine rumbling to life as I pulled onto the road. The quiet charm of River Bend blurred past —white picket fences, a roadside café, and the occasional historic home. The late morning sun glinted off the river in the distance, its calm surface mocking the storm inside me. The farther I drove, the more the scenery transformed. Rolling hills and vibrant trees faded into highways and overpasses, the hum of traffic pressing in as the city got closer.

Somewhere along the way, my phone buzzed on the dashboard mount. My father's name lit up the screen, glaring at me like an accusation.

I ignored it.

He called again a minute later. Then again. And again.

By the fourth call, I knew I couldn't avoid him. A familiar pressure settled in my chest like a stone as I tightened my grip on the wheel. My father wasn't a man you ignored without consequences, and the Ashworths' anger had only fueled his determination.

Steeling myself, I pressed the button on the steering wheel to answer.

"Father."

"Henry," he said, his voice as cold and sharp as a blade. "I've had about enough of your games. Care to explain what the hell happened yesterday morning?"

I gritted my teeth, my knuckles whitening on the wheel. "If this is about Caroline, she decided. There was nothing I could do."

"Don't lie to me," he snapped, his words slicing through the air like a whip. "I know you were supposed to propose. What I don't know is why the hell that Honeysucker girl was there."

My stomach dropped. I forced myself to breathe evenly. "What are you talking about?"

"Don't insult my intelligence," he said, his voice cold and clipped. "I had someone follow you. Imagine my surprise when the person meeting with you wasn't Caroline herself, but Savannah Honeysucker—your old distraction from River Bend."

A chill ran down my spine. "Father, I—"

"Spare me your excuses," he snapped, his anger sharp and cutting. "What reason could that girl have for being there? Is this why you've dragged your feet on this proposal? Because you've been pining over that low-class fantasy all these years?"

"That's not what happened," I said, my voice louder than I intended. "Savvy was there because Caroline hired her. That's her job—she ends relationships for a living."

There was a pause, heavy and calculating. "Caroline hired her?"

"Yes," I said quickly, desperate to steer the conversation away from dangerous territory. "She didn't want to marry me, and instead of telling me herself, she paid someone to do it."

He scoffed. "And you let it happen? Do you have any idea how ridiculous this makes you look? Humiliated by Caroline and tangled up with that Honeysucker girl again." His voice dripped with disdain. "You're a Kingston, Henry. Start acting like it."

"I'm not tangled up with anyone," I said, the lie sour on my tongue. "Savvy was doing her job."

"Then she'd better stay far away from anything involving this family," he said. "Because if she crosses us again, I'll make sure her little business—and her family—regret it."

A wave of panic surged through me. "Leave her out of this," I said, my voice low and steady. "She had nothing to do with it. Caroline didn't want to marry me, and that's all there is to it."

"That's all?" he repeated, his voice cold and mocking. "The Ashworths are calling for answers. You'll fix this by the end of the week."

"I told you, there's nothing to fix. It's over."

"You'll smooth things out," he said with finality. "Or I'll destroy the Honeysuckers for ruining what I built."

The line went dead, leaving an icy knot of dread in its wake. Tossing the phone onto the passenger seat, I let out a shaky breath. My father was a master of wielding power as a weapon, and now that Savvy had re-entered the picture, I knew he would aim it straight at her if it suited his purposes.

My father's threats sat heavy in my chest as I drove the rest of the way to Madison Center. When I stepped into my grandfather's room, I tried to keep my expression calm, though it was clear today wasn't one of his good days. His usually vibrant eyes were dull, and his gaze seemed far away, fixed on the garden beyond the window.

"Grandfather," I greeted softly, taking the seat beside him.

He turned toward me slowly, his gaze searching my face. I thought I saw a spark of recognition for a moment, but it vanished as quickly as it came. "And you are?" he asked, his voice uncertain.

My stomach clenched. "It's me. I'm Henry, your grandson." I reached out and placed my hand over his. "I came to check on you."

His fingers curled slightly under mine, but he didn't pull away. "I'm glad you're here," he murmured, his gaze drifting back to the window. "It's so quiet in this place. Too quiet."

I looked out at the manicured gardens, the vibrant fall colors doing little to lift the heaviness in the air. "I spoke to her, Grandfather," I ventured after a moment. "Savvy. She said she'd come to see you."

His brow furrowed as he processed the name. "Savvy," he repeated slowly, testing it out. Then, with a tilt of his head, he said, "Who is that?"

I cleared my throat, struggling to keep my voice steady. "She's ... someone important. Someone who means a lot to both of us."

"Hmm." He didn't seem convinced, but his focus drifted again. "It's nice out there today," he said, nodding toward the garden. "The trees ... the colors..."

I nodded, swallowing the lump in my throat. "Yes, they're beautiful."

We sat in silence for a while, the quiet broken only by the distant hum of activity in the hallway. I wanted to tell him more, to reassure him that Savvy would come, but the words didn't come. Would she keep her promise? Or was I setting him—and myself—up for disappointment?

The sound of a nurse entering pulled me out of my thoughts. She offered me a small, sympathetic look as she approached. "Mr. Morrison, it's time for your medication and a nap."

My grandfather sighed heavily, his usual spark of resistance dimming. "All right, all right," he muttered. As the nurse helped him take his pills, he looked back at me, his gaze momentarily sharper. "Henry," he said, his voice carrying a note of clarity. "She's coming, isn't she?"

The question surprised me, and for a moment, I froze. Then, summoning more confidence than I had, I nodded. "She's visiting you today, Grandfather."

His expression changed, the warmth I remembered glimmering back into his eyes. "Good," he said. "I'd like to see her."

As I left the Madison Center, his words echoed in my mind, filling me with hope and dread. Savvy had said she would come, but would she?

CHAPTER TEN

Savvy

The train ride to Madison Center stretched endlessly
before me, each mile a reminder of the control I was
choosing to relinquish. I'd cleared my calendar for the next
few days, a rash decision made without fully understanding
why. It wasn't like me to leave loose ends, but after yesterday, I couldn't trust myself to keep delivering perfect good-
byes. Three hundred and forty-two flawless endings, yet all
it had taken was one look at Henry Kingston to unravel me.

The trip gave me seventy-five minutes to question
everything—coming alone, the last five years of my life.
Manhattan's skyline loomed ahead, sharp and glittering, like
a crown of thorns. It was Henry's world. One I'd always
circled but never touched. In that world, I'd made a name
for myself by being his opposite: the kind of person who
could walk away without leaving a piece of herself behind.

When I stepped off the train, the late afternoon air had
that particular Manhattan crispness that usually centered
me before a job. Not today. Today, my professional distance

felt like tissue paper in a storm. I couldn't stop replaying yesterday's scene—the way my voice had cracked on his name, the raw edge in my tone as I delivered Caroline's goodbye, the moment years of perfect composure had shattered like cheap glass.

Madison Center loomed ahead, all gleaming glass and modern angles—nothing like the architecture that Henry and I used to admire along River Bend's waterfront. Inside, the warmth hit me like a wall, and I shrugged off my jacket, the soft cashmere sweater beneath chosen with deliberate thought. It was comfortable without looking careless, saying, "I'm doing fine," without trying too hard to prove it.

The lobby radiated calculated comfort—polished floors gleaming like a magazine cover, a receptionist with an air of professional charm, and chairs designed to suggest luxury without overstaying your welcome. A piano rendition of "Moon River" floated through the air, subtle enough to feel elegant but prominent enough to ensure you noticed it.

I fought back a laugh. Of course, they'd put Henry's grandfather in a place where even the background music seemed deliberate.

"Can I help you?" The receptionist's expression was poised and polished, everything I used to be before yesterday.

"I'm here to see James Morrison." The words felt foreign on my tongue. "Savannah Honeysucker."

Recognition passed across her face. "Ah, yes. Mr. Kingston mentioned you'd be coming."

Mr. Kingston. Not Henry—only one Kingston commanded that kind of automatic respect. My stomach twisted. "Henry's father knows I'm here?"

"Oh, no." She typed something into her computer. "The

youngest Kingston. He added you to the approved visitor list before he left earlier today."

The knot in my stomach loosened. Of course, Henry would think of that. He'd been good at the little details, at smoothing the way for others. It was one of the first things I'd loved about him, back when I was young enough to mistake thoughtfulness for forever.

"Room 517," she said, handing me a visitor's badge. "The elevator's around the corner. Would you like someone to show you—"

"I can find it." The words came out sharper than I intended. It was Jennifer Walsh's professional distance bleeding into Savvy's emotions again.

The ride gave me several floors to second-guess everything—the years I'd spent trying to move on, the decision to come here. The numbers ticked up with mechanical precision as memories surged forward. James taught me chess in his study, sharing rare first editions he knew I'd cherish, standing up for me to his son-in-law with quiet, unyielding dignity.

The doors opened onto a hallway that looked more like a luxury hotel than a medical facility. Plush carpeting muffled my steps as I followed the numbers: 511, 513, 515...

I paused outside 517, my hand half-raised to knock when James's voice drifted through the partially open door. "Are you going to stand there all day? Or have you developed a sudden fascination with hospital decor?"

A laugh escaped before I could stop it. Pushing the door open, I stepped into a room that was pure James—floor-to-ceiling windows overlooking manicured gardens, leather armchairs that probably cost more than my monthly student loan payment, and books. So many books, their spines creating a familiar rainbow against the pristine walls.

He sat in one of those ridiculously expensive chairs, a worn copy of *The Great Gatsby* open on his lap. He looked smaller than I remembered, more fragile, but his eyes still held that sharp intelligence that had seen right through everyone's pretenses.

"Savannah Rose," he said, and for a moment, I saw the man who'd spent hours discussing literature with me in his study. "You still have that look when you're overthinking things."

"Old habits." I stepped closer, taking in the changes time had etched into him. His hair was completely white now, his face marked with lines that told stories of more than just years. But the way he looked at me hadn't changed —still warm and knowing, as if he were in on some cosmic joke the rest of us had yet to understand.

"Sit." He gestured to the chair beside him. "Before you wear a hole in my expensive carpet with all that nervous energy."

I sank into the leather chair, its softness both comforting and a little unnerving. James and the books seemed to hum with memories I'd tried to forget, stirring something I didn't want to face. I fidgeted in my seat, trying to shake it off. "Henry said you wanted to see me, Mr. Morrison."

"Mr. Morrison?" His eyebrow arched as he marked his place and closed the book. "Five years and suddenly we're strangers, Savannah Rose? You might be the Goodbye Girl to everyone else, but you don't get to say goodbye so fast to me."

The use of my full name and the jab at my career sent a pang through my chest. No one in Manhattan knew

Jennifer Walsh's real identity outside my close friends and family—no one except Henry.

"You look good." He studied me with those sharp eyes that had seen too much. "Harder, maybe. More guarded. But good."

"I'm fine." The words came automatically, my standard response to any inquiry about my emotional state. The exact words I'd practiced in the mirror until they sounded believable, until I could deliver them without flinching.

"What happened to the wedding planner dream?" James asked, tilting his head. "You always said you'd plan happily-ever-afters for a living."

I let out a soft laugh, the kind that sticks in your throat. "Things changed, and I went in the opposite direction."

His eyebrow lifted, curiosity sparking in his eyes. "I'd say. Explain this to me."

"I, uh..." Heat crawled up my neck. "I help people end relationships."

"End relationships?" His voice was even, but his expression betrayed a hint of surprise.

"Yep. I'm the one they call when things get ... messy," I admitted, my hands twisting in my lap. "Quietly, efficiently, and without attaching my name to it."

James regarded me momentarily, something close to amusement glinting in his eyes. "Not quite what you planned when you used to sit in my study dreaming about your future, is it?"

"Nope, but dreams rarely turn into reality." I tried to sound steady, but calm slipped away, impossible to grasp here. The room was styled like a den—cozy armchairs, a wooden bookshelf, muted lighting—but it wasn't his den. It lacked the warmth and history of the study where I used to sit, dreaming about a future that now seemed like a lifetime ago. I glanced at him, searching for a piece of the person I used to know. "People change, too."

"Do they?" His gaze sharpened. "Or do they get better at hiding who they are?"

"James—"

"Did you know Henry comes to visit me every day?" The abrupt change of subject knocked me off balance. "Even on the bad days, when I don't remember who he is."

My throat tightened. "I didn't know you were having bad days."

"More and more lately, I'm told." He let out a quiet breath, the weariness settling into his features. "The mind is a funny thing, Savannah. Some days, I remember every-thing—every book I've read, every deal I've made, every moment with Margaret." His voice grew quiet at the mention of his late wife. "And other days ... I look at my grandson and see a stranger."

"I'm sorry." The words slipped out in Savvy's raw, unguarded voice, not Jennifer's polished tones. "I didn't know."

"Nobody knows. That's how I wanted it." He picked up his book, running his fingers over the worn cover. "Did you ever read this?"

"Gatsby?" I latched onto the familiar territory of literary discussion, which belonged to the old me, not the profes-sional I'd become. "It was required reading in high school."

"Ah, but did you *read* it?" His eyes took on that familiar gleam he used to get when we discussed literature. "Really read it, not just for a grade?"

"I..." I hesitated, remembering countless discussions in his study. "I thought it was a warning about the danger of living in the past."

"Close." He set the book aside. "It's about trying to

recreate the past. Of thinking you can go back and fix what's broken instead of building something new from the pieces."

Understanding hit me like a physical blow. "James—"

"Henry told me what happened with Caroline." His voice carried a touch of amusement. "Quite the coincidence, wouldn't you say? You being the one to deliver that message?"

"It was just business." But even I could hear the lie in my voice.

"Was it?" He leaned forward. "Or was it the universe's way of saying some stories aren't finished yet?"

"Our story is finished." The words came out sharper than I intended. "Henry made that very clear five years ago."

"Did he?" James's expression turned thoughtful. "Or did you both assume you knew what the other was thinking? That's the trouble with young love—everyone's so busy protecting themselves that they forget to actually talk to each other."

"There wasn't much talking involved." I couldn't keep the edge from my voice. "He just ... disappeared."

"Ah." James nodded slowly. "Like Gatsby disappeared from Daisy's life? To protect her? To become worthy?"

"This isn't a novel." I stood, needing to put distance between myself and his too-perceptive gaze. "Henry didn't leave to become worthy. He left because—" I stopped, realizing I still didn't know why. All those years, and I'd never gotten an explanation.

"Because he thought he was protecting you," James said gently, his voice steady but soft. "The same way I would have protected Margaret from anything—even myself if I had to."

I turned to face him, my heart pounding. "What are you talking about?"

"Henry never stopped loving you, Savannah." The words struck deep, knocking the breath from my lungs. "He walked away to keep you safe, even if it meant losing you. That's not so hard to understand, is it?"

"That's not—" My voice cracked. "He didn't—"

"Didn't he?" James picked up his book again, though his gaze stayed locked on me. "My son-in-law can be ... persuasive when he wants something. And what he wanted was for Henry to be the perfect Kingston heir. No distractions. No small-town girlfriends with dreams that didn't fit the family image."

The room seemed to tilt. "What are you saying?"

"I'm saying that sometimes the people we love make terrible choices for the right reasons." His expression turned somber. "And sometimes the right reasons aren't enough to justify the pain they cause."

I sank back into the chair, my legs suddenly unable to hold me up. "Henry's father ... threatened him?"

"He did more than threaten," James said, his voice laced with old anger. "He prepared everything in advance— manipulating property assessments, building inspection reports, creating a paper trail that could make the marina look like a failing business whenever he needed it. Richard doesn't just destroy things, Savannah. He establishes the mechanism for destruction, ready to deploy at a moment's notice. Makes it look like he's three steps ahead, ready to be the executioner."

I stood abruptly, anger and hurt warring inside me. "I'm not surprised Richard Kingston would try to control everyone's lives," I said, my voice tight. "But I am surprised Henry let him."

James watched me pace, his eyes tracking my movement. "What would you have done if he'd told you?"

"Henry could have told me. We could have—"

"What?" James's voice was calm, almost too calm. "Fought back? Against a man who controls half of Manhattan's real estate? Who could buy and sell River Bend ten times over without blinking?" He shook his head slowly. "Henry was young. Inexperienced. He did what he thought would protect you. Was it the right choice? Probably not. But it was the only one he thought he had."

Memories flooded back—the way Henry had seemed distant in those last few weeks, the unease that crept in whenever his father was mentioned, the way he'd looked at me like he was memorizing my face.

"I've missed our talks." James's voice pulled me back to the present. "The way you see straight to the heart of things. The way you made Henry laugh—really laugh, not that polite society chuckle he uses now."

"James—"

"I have little time left." He said it matter-of-factly, like commenting on the weather. "And I think about regret. About all the things we leave unsaid because we're too proud or too scared or too certain we know what's best for everyone else."

I swallowed past the lump in my throat. "What are you saying?"

"I'm saying that sometimes the universe gives us second chances." He reached for my hand, his grip surprisingly strong. "And sometimes those chances come disguised as professional obligations, family requests, or coincidences that aren't coincidences at all."

"I can't—" I took a shaky breath. "I can't forget everything that happened."

"Of course not. And you shouldn't." He squeezed my hand. "But maybe you can try to understand it. To see that sometimes the people we love make mistakes because they love us too much, not too little."

A nurse appeared in the doorway. "Mr. Morrison? It's time for your dinner."

James sighed with familiar exasperation. "The warden approaches." But his eyes stayed on me, sharp and knowing. "Will you come back?"

The question caught me off guard. "I—"

"Not for Henry," he added quickly. "For me. I've missed having someone to discuss books with who reads them for pleasure, not status."

I looked at this man who'd been more of a grandfather to me than either of my own, who'd defended me to his family, who'd seen past my small-town roots to recognize a kindred spirit.

"I'll think about it."

The way his face lit up was worth any awkwardness this might cause. "Good," he said as if it were a done deal. "Bring that copy of *Jane Eyre* we were arguing about last time. I still say Rochester was an idiot."

"He was trying to protect Jane," I said automatically, falling into our old pattern.

"By lying to her?"

James's eyebrows rose. "By making choices for her without giving her all the information?" he asked.

The parallel wasn't lost on me. "That's not—"

"Same time tomorrow?" He was reaching for his book again, dismissing me with the casual authority of someone used to ending conversations on his terms.

I stood, smoothing my sweater with my hands. "Same time tomorrow."

At the door, I turned back. James was silhouetted against the window, the golden light framing him in shades of shadow. He looked smaller somehow, more fragile, but his voice was strong when he called out:

"Savannah?"

"Yes?"

"Sometimes the bravest thing we can do is admit we might have been wrong about why something happened." He held my gaze, his expression unreadable—yet knowing, as always. "Even if we were right about how much it hurt."

I left Madison Center with my head spinning and my heart aching in ways I thought I'd buried years ago. The Hudson reflected streaks of pink and gold, reminding me of countless evenings on the dock with Henry.

Checking my phone, I saw it was after four. I'd made it out in time.

My phone buzzed.

HENRY

On my way. Traffic's light, so I might be early.

My heart jumped. After years of silence, and now here he was, casually texting me like no time had passed. Like he hadn't shattered everything we'd built.

ME

I've already left.

HENRY

Savvy, wait. Please.

ME

I need space.

I shoved my phone into my bag after turning it to silent

—only to see the faint glow of the screen through the fabric as a message came in.

MADDY

How did it go?

IVY

Are you okay? Do you need us?

ME

I don't know. James told me something about why Henry left.

MADDY

WHAT???

IVY

We're on our way. Where are you?

ME

No. Really. I need to process this alone.

MADDY

Since when have you processed anything alone?

IVY

She's running from Henry, isn't she?

ME

I'm not running. I'm being tactical.

MADDY

Same difference with you.

They weren't wrong. I was running—from Henry, from James's revelations, from how I crumbled every time Henry looked at me with those eyes that still saw straight to my soul.

CHAPTER ELEVEN

Henry

When I walked into my grandfather's room at Madison Center, the evening light filtered through the blinds, casting striped patterns across the medical equipment he despised. He sat in his usual chair by the window, but something about his posture was different—more alert, more present.

"You missed her," he said without turning around.

"I know." I sank into the chair beside him. "She made it clear she needed space."

"Can't blame her." He looked at me, his eyes sharp with one of his good moments. "Finding out why you left ... that's quite a burden to process."

My stomach dropped. "What did you tell her?"

"The truth. All of it. Your father's threats, the choice you made, everything." No apology in his voice, just calm certainty.

"That wasn't your story to tell." The words came out harder than I intended.

"You had five years to tell it yourself." His gaze didn't waver. "Five years and you chose silence."

Before I could respond, my phone buzzed. *Father. Again.* I sent it to voicemail, but it immediately rang again. Something cold settled in my stomach as I answered.

"Henry." My father's voice held that infuriating edge that signaled he'd won whatever game he'd played. "I trust you've heard about River Bend Books?"

My head snapped up. "What about it?"

"Such a shame. All those building code violations suddenly came to light. The inspector's report landed on my desk. Foundation issues, electrical problems, potential fire hazards..." He paused for effect. "They'll have to close immediately, of course. Safety first." He chuckled. "And that little apartment above the store? Also, uninhabitable. Savvy will need to find new accommodations. Immediately."

The room tilted. "You can't—"

"I can, and I have. Consider it a warning shot." There was a pause, followed by the distinct sound of ice cubes clinking against crystal. Henry knew his father's habits well enough—he'd be in his study now, drinking that 50-year-old Macallan he saved for moments of triumph. "The marina deal is next. Unless..."

"Unless what?"

"Unless you fix things with Caroline. Immediately." Another pause. "The Ashworths can be persuaded back to the table. Make her see reason, Henry. Get that ring on her finger. Whatever it takes."

My grandfather's hand found my arm, his grip surprisingly strong. I covered the phone. "He's going after the bookstore first."

Understanding flashed in his eyes. He reached for his

tablet on the side table, fingers moving with surprising speed across the screen. "Linda," he called to his nurse. "I need you to call Charles Barrett at Morrison Trust. Tell him it's urgent."

I uncovered the phone. "I'll call you back."

"You have one hour to decide," my father said. "Before I file those inspection reports."

The line went dead as Linda stepped out to make the call. Not even thirty seconds later, my phone buzzed.

MASON

Warning—your father's prepped the inspection reports. They're queued to file.

My grandfather continued working on his tablet, his face set in lines of concentration I hadn't seen in months.

"You can't access your accounts," I said. "Father made sure of that after your diagnosis."

"Your father," he said without looking up, "forgets who taught him how to build an empire." He handed me the tablet. "Look."

On the screen was a trust document I'd never seen before, dated after my grandmother died. It included properties, accounts, and, most importantly, allies. The document also listed the names of people who owed James Morrison favors, people my father had overlooked or dismissed.

"The building that houses River Bend Books?" His lips curved, but it wasn't his usual warm expression. This was the calculated grin that had made him a legend in New York real estate. "Your father thinks he controls everything in this city. But he forgot that genuine power isn't about what you own—it's about who you know."

My phone buzzed again.

MASON

He filed them. Moving faster than he
threatened.

"He's not even waiting the hour," I said, anger rising.
"He's not bluffing about closing the store."

"No." My grandfather took his phone from Linda as she
returned. "He never bluffs. But neither do I." Into the
phone, he said, "Charles? James Morrison. Remember
when you helped my daughter plan her wedding? And I
helped your son get into Yale? I need a favor..."

I watched in awe for the next forty minutes as James
Morrison dismantled my father's plan with nothing but a
phone and forty years of meticulously nurtured relationships. Every time my father's name appeared on my phone,
another call went out from my grandfather's.

"Your father," James said between calls, "never understood the difference between being feared and being
respected." He gestured to the tablet. "Look at the names,
Henry. Really look at them."

I scrolled through the list—building inspectors, city
council members, bank executives, but also doormen, secre-
taries, and maintenance workers—people my father would
have dismissed as irrelevant, but James had treated them as
equals.

"Sandra Martinez," I read aloud. "Isn't she—"

"The woman who cleaned my office for twenty years?
Yes." He leaned back, a calculated ease in his posture. "And
her daughter now heads the city's building inspection
department. Funny how life works, isn't it?"

He set the phone down. "The inspection reports have
been ... temporarily misplaced. The review board is
suddenly jam-packed." He leaned back, his focus shifting to

the window as his expression grew more thoughtful. "I've had years to plan for this," he said, a trace of exhaustion evident in his voice. "Ever since you walked away from that girl to protect her, I knew your father would eventually make his move.

"The marina will be harder—he's had more time to fortify his position there. But the bookstore?" He closed his eyes briefly, as though bracing himself. "Consider it a down payment on my apology for not stopping him sooner."

I stared at him. For a moment, I couldn't speak. The man who'd spent most of my life building and strategizing, who had been ahead of everyone, was still in there. Beneath the weariness and years of battling a diagnosis that had stolen so much, he was still fighting—for me.

"Thank you," I said, the words catching in my throat. Gratitude wasn't enough for what he was doing, for what this moment meant, but it was all I could manage.

He nodded. "I wasn't going to let him win, Henry. Not this time."

For the first time in years, I experienced a glimmer of hope. "Tell me about the marina deal," I said, leaning forward. "What exactly has my father set up?"

"Ah." James's eyes took on that sharp focus that meant he was fully present, his mind as sharp as ever. "Your father's had his eye on that marina. He's had people working for him—or paying off assessors—to keep the property undervalued. When the time was right, he planned to scoop it up for a song."

My stomach churned. "So, when he swoops in with an offer—"

"It looks like he's doing Paul Honeysucker a favor." James nodded. "Offering above market value for a 'struggling' business. On paper, it's perfect. Clean. Undisputable."

"But the marina's not struggling. I've seen their books." The memory hit hard—Savvy showing me the ledgers with pride, explaining how they'd modernized the accounting system while keeping her grandfather's old business principles. "They were doing better than ever."

"It doesn't matter what's true." James's voice carried a note of sadness. "Only what the paperwork says. And your father's had five years to make the paperwork tell exactly the story he wants it to tell."

My phone buzzed. Mason again.

MASON

> Your father's called an emergency board
> meeting for tomorrow morning—9 a.m.

"He's moving faster than I expected," James said, reading the message over my shoulder. "Good. That means we've rattled him."

"How is that good?"

"Because Richard makes mistakes when he's angry. When things don't go according to his perfect plans." A trace of that shrewd businessman showed in James's expression. "And right now, he's furious."

Through the window, in the distance, Manhattan's lights began twinkling on, a constellation of power and money that had seemed so far from River Bend's quiet charm. I'd spent years trying to bridge those two worlds, never realizing that my grandfather had built those bridges, one relationship at a time.

"About Savvy," I said. "What exactly did you tell her?"

"Everything you should have told her yourself." No

softening of the blow. "About Richard's threats. About the choice you made. About why you walked away."

"I was protecting her."

"No." His voice gentled. "You were protecting yourself. From having to watch her fight back. From seeing her choose a battle you thought she couldn't win."

"She would have lost everything."

"Maybe." He adjusted his blanket, his movements deliberate. "Or maybe she would have surprised you. She surprised me today by sitting in that chair where you are now, hearing the truth and not breaking. Just getting stronger." His gaze met mine. "The way she's surprised everyone by building a life after you left—not the one she planned, but her own kind of determination."

"How did she take it?"

"She said," James added with a tilt of his head, "that she wasn't surprised Richard Kingston would try to control everyone's lives. But she was surprised you let him."

The words cut through me, sharp and unyielding. Because that was Savvy—she never hesitated to strip away the layers, exposing the raw, undeniable truth. I had let my father dictate our lives, all while convincing myself I was safeguarding her.

"I'm an idiot," I whispered.

"Yes." James's agreement came quickly. "But you're an idiot who's ready to fight back. That's something." He closed his eyes briefly. "Now the question is, what will you do about it?"

I looked down at the tablet. "I'm going to fix it."

"No." His voice sharpened. "You're going to help her fix it. There's a difference." He reached for his phone one last time. "Which is why there's one more call I have to make."

I watched as he dialed a number from memory, his fingers moving with practiced ease.

"Paul?" he said after a moment. "James Morrison. Yes, it's been too long. Listen, I need to tell you something about a potential offer for the marina..."

I sat there as my grandfather laid out the entire story—Richard's efforts to manipulate property values and pressure Paul Honeysucker into selling. Paul's responses were too quiet for me to hear, but the tight set of James's jaw and the subtle shifts in his expression told me everything I needed to know.

When he hung up, he looked drained but satisfied. "Well, that's done."

"What did he say?" I asked, leaning forward.

James rubbed a hand over his face. "He said, 'Leave the marina to me. But you tell that grandson of yours something for me.'"

I stilled, waiting.

"He said, 'My daughter needs to hear all this from him —not from me. And tell him it's about damn time he fought for her.'"

The words lingered, sharp and undeniable. Fought for her. I'd spent so long convincing myself that walking away was the best way to protect her, but maybe it was the easiest. James was right. It was time—past time. I wasn't about to let my father win. Not this time.

James's eyes clouded, the good moment fading. "Go," he said. "You have a board meeting to prepare for, and I'm exhausted."

I stood, gathering the tablet and the files he'd shared. It wasn't mine to take, but its data was crucial—and James knew it as well as I did. "Thank you. For everything."

"Don't thank me yet." His voice was growing fainter. "Just remember something for me, Henry."

"Anything."

"Your father thinks love is weakness. That it makes you vulnerable, gives people power over you." His eyes drifted closed. "But genuine love? The kind that makes you fight even when you might lose? That's the strongest power there is."

I watched him sink deeper into his chair, today's burst of energy taking its toll. Tomorrow would bring the board meeting, my father's rage, and god only knew what else. But tonight, seeing the spark Savvy had brought back to my grandfather's eyes, I understood what real strength looked like.

The lights of Manhattan winked at me as I gathered my things. Somewhere out there, my father was plotting his next move, believing money and fear could solve any problem.

But seeing how Savvy's visit had transformed my grandfather, even for a few hours, I realized there might still be a way to protect everyone I loved. I had to convince her to trust me one more time.

I pulled out my phone, staring at her number. A silence that spanned half a decade, and now I was about to ask for the impossible. The irony wasn't lost on me—I'd left to protect her, and she'd built a career around leaving to protect herself.

Maybe it was time we both figured out how to stay.

CHAPTER TWELVE

Savvy

The train ride home from Madison Center seemed longer than usual, each mile marker a reminder of how thoroughly my world had turned. James's words kept echoing in my head. "Richard Kingston doesn't make empty threats."

Five years. For five years, I'd told myself a story about not being enough, about Henry choosing his perfect world over our messy love. I'd built an entire career around that story. Around delivering the clean breaks I never got.

But Henry hadn't walked away because he didn't care enough. He'd walked away because he cared too much—because his father had spent weeks laying out exactly how he could destroy everything my family had built. Still, he should have told me. He should have trusted me enough to let me decide how much I could handle, instead of deciding for both of us.

I pulled out my business phone, the one reserved for client contact. No new requests. Then my personal phone buzzed with a text from Dr. Blake.

DR. BLAKE

We need to discuss your recent client cancellations. Without consistent proof of your professional reliability, I can't continue referring people to your services.

My stomach dropped. Dr. Blake's referrals made up nearly half of my income. She was the reason Manhattan's elite trusted my professional alias with their delicate matters in the first place. Without her stamp of approval, I might as well apply for a barista job at Common Grounds.

Three hundred and forty-two perfect goodbyes, and then there was Henry Kingston—number three hundred and forty-three. It had taken one look at him to shatter my reputation. No wonder she was questioning my reliability.

I typed and deleted three different responses to Dr. Blake before settling on: "I've had a personal matter come up. It won't affect my future performance." But even I didn't believe that anymore.

"You're not in your usual spot." Joe appeared with his usual tissue box.

I waved it away. "Sometimes we need to view life from another angle." My voice sounded strange, hollow. "Just sitting here processing."

"Processing looks an awful lot like overthinking from where I'm standing."

I let out a soft chuckle. "Occupational hazard."

He patted me on the shoulder and walked away.

My mind kept circling back to James's words. Richard Kingston had laid the groundwork years ago to destroy my family. The research was done; the plans were made, and I'd given him the perfect reason to act by delivering Caroline's goodbye.

My phone lit up. Dr. Blake's name flashed through my

mind, but an NYU student loan notice glared back at me, the numbers a stark reminder of the life I'd planned versus the one I'd built. At least the breakup broker business kept the collectors at bay. Who knew helping people end relationships could pay so well? Or that I'd be good at it?

The screen lit up again. Henry. Seeing his name sent a wave of emotions crashing through me—anger, regret, and something else I refused to acknowledge. His timing was impeccable, wasn't it? Showing up when I was regaining my balance, when the business was starting to feel solid. His family had a way of wrecking everything they touched, their wealth a wrecking ball disguised in silk.

I checked my business phone out of habit—no new clients. The irony wasn't lost on me. I'd built a career helping others walk away cleanly from messy relationships, yet here I was, still tangled in the threads of my past. The phone was heavy in my hand, Henry's name still glowing on the screen like a warning sign I was choosing to ignore.

The train lurched around a bend, and I caught my reflection in the darkened window. The perfectly-styled hair, the professional blazer, the mask of composure I'd worked so hard to perfect—none of it was real anymore. Jennifer Walsh, the untouchable breakup broker, had been built on believing Henry Kingston hadn't cared enough. Now that foundation was gone, replaced by something far more complicated.

My phone lit up again—Henry's number. I let it ring.

The train pulled into River Bend Station as the sun was setting. Main Street stretched ahead, the familiar walk home suddenly feeling longer than usual. The Weathered Barn's windows were dark, Mr. Dixon having closed at five on the dot. Mrs. Patterson was probably updating her neighborhood watch group about my return—she never missed a detail.

My phone buzzed again. Henry.

I ignored it as I passed Common Grounds, Cork & Crown, the post office—each storefront a reminder of the life Henry and I had shared, the life his father had threatened. When I rounded the corner to River Bend Books, I stopped short.

Through the windows, I could see lights still on despite the "Closed" sign. And there, behind the counter where Mom usually stood, was Dad—looking as out of place as an engine manual in the poetry section. The fluorescent lights caught the silver in his hair and the worry lines around his eyes, making him seem older than I'd ever seen him.

I froze. In twenty years, I'd never seen my father leave the marina early. The man had shown up to my college graduation with engine grease under his nails and a socket wrench in his pocket, swearing he'd be back at the garage before the last dipstick had time to cool. Seeing him here, among Mom's shelves and literary treasures, sent a chill down my spine that had nothing to do with the evening air.

My phone buzzed as I reached for the door handle. Henry could wait. The sight of my father anywhere but the marina at this time of day meant something had happened—something big enough to drag him away from Mrs. Mitchell's temperamental Volvo and Old Joe's ancient Chris-Craft. This has to be about what happened earlier today.

The bell above the shop door chimed as I stepped inside, the familiar sound suddenly feeling more like a warning than a welcome. The usual comforting scent of paper and binding glue mixed with something foreign— motor oil and worry.

Books surrounded me in their familiar rainbow rows, their spines creating the kind of comfort only well-loved stories can provide. The romance section caught my eye—or rather, I caught myself avoiding it, the way I had since Henry left. Mom still ordered the latest releases, arranged them with care, probably hoping one day I'd stop wincing at happy endings. Tonight, even the cheerful covers seemed to mock the unease in the air.

"Savannah." Mom's voice had that undercurrent she reserved for delivering bad news—the same one she'd used to tell me our ancient tabby, Marmalade, wouldn't be coming home from the vet. Her fingers fidgeted with the reading glasses hanging from their chain around her neck, a nervous habit I hadn't seen since the last time the rent went up. "Your father had a phone call today."

Dad turned, and I saw grease stains on Mom's pristine counter for the first time in my life. Paul Honeysucker might live and breathe engines, but he'd never bring marina grime into Mom's literary sanctuary. Not unless something had rattled him enough to forget his own rules. The smudges looked like black butterflies against the polished wood, each one marking a moment his hands had clenched and unclenched while he waited.

"The building inspector came by," he said, his voice holding something dark. "Found some interesting problems that weren't there last month." The words came out like they'd been caught in a failing transmission, grinding against each other.

"Interesting." The word tasted foreign, off somehow. After what James had told me about Richard Kingston's plans, 'interesting' was about as fitting as calling a hurricane a light breeze. "What problems?"

"Electrical issues." Dad's hands clutched the edge of the

counter. "Foundation concerns. Violations that could shut down a business or move you out of your home." He paused, his following words careful, each measured like he was adjusting a delicate valve. "The problems that appear right after someone powerful makes them appear."

My phone buzzed again—Henry.

"When did this happen?" I tried to keep my voice steady, but it wavered like a boat in choppy waters.

"About an hour ago." Dad's fingers drummed against the counter, leaving tiny grease prints like morse code. "Walked through the whole place like he knew what he was looking for. Said we'd have to close immediately, that you'd need to move out of the apartment—"

"But then James Morrison called." Mom's cardigan was practically a straitjacket now, wrapped so tight I wondered if she was trying to hold herself together or stop herself from throwing things. She paced behind the counter, her sensible shoes clicking against the hardwood in an anxious rhythm. "Said not to worry about the orders yet. That he was ... handling things."

"Handling things?" The words came out awkward and unfamiliar, like trying to read a book in the dark.

"He said to sit tight until we hear from his contacts." Dad's voice held equal parts worry and wonder. "Something about building department records getting temporarily misplaced." His weathered hands spread flat on the counter now as if bracing himself for impact.

"And then he told us everything else." Mom's hands twisted in her cardigan, her wedding ring catching the light with each nervous movement. "About Richard Kingston's threats five years ago. About why Henry left. About—"

"His father threatened to destroy everything if he

didn't," I finished for her. "I know. James told me today. That's where I was—at Madison Center."

Dad's eyes met Mom's over my head, one of those silent conversations they'd perfected over thirty years of marriage. The kind that usually preceded either good news or bad news. And given that Dad was at the bookstore instead of fixing Mrs. Mitchell's Volvo, I had a pretty good guess which this was. The air between them seemed to crackle with unvoiced concerns and shared fears.

My phone lit up again. Henry.

"You should probably answer that," Dad said, his voice low—the same one he used when telling customers their engines were beyond saving. Steady, careful, meant to cushion the impact. He hesitated, then added, even gentler, "You've heard James's side. Maybe it's time to hear it from the source."

I exhaled slowly, forcing the knot in my chest to loosen. I wasn't ready to face him but avoiding him hadn't solved anything. The silence between us had stretched too far, and now it threatened to snap. My head shouted no, insisting I keep my distance, but that small, stubborn piece of my heart he still owned whispered yes.

Maybe I didn't have all the answers, but I knew one thing: I couldn't keep running from this. I wasn't letting him back into my life—I was just getting the details on why he left. That was it. I didn't have to be open or kind or even civil. I just needed to hear what he had to say and take it one minute at a time. Or so I told myself.

CHAPTER THIRTEEN

Henry

Fifth call. Still no answer.

I sat in my car outside Madison Center, the glow from the screen throwing streaks of light across the dashboard. My call history showed five attempts, each ending in the same dead air. My thumb hovered over her name again, my grandfather's words from earlier settling over me like a lead blanket.

Of course, she was—after all these years of silence, what right did I have to expect anything else?

But I couldn't stop. Not now. Not after what James told me—what I saw this morning.

I pressed redial. Sixth call.

The line rung once. Twice. I braced for the click of voicemail, the inevitable defeat. Then, a voice.

"Hello?"

I froze. Her voice was cautious and neutral. My heart kicked into overdrive, pounding in my ears like an alarm.

"Savvy, it's me," I said before she could hang up.

There was a pause, sharp and deliberate. "What do you want, Henry?" Her voice was clipped—she wasn't interested in pleasantries.

"Please, don't hang up," I blurted. My grip on the steering wheel tightened. "This is important."

Another pause. I could practically hear her weighing her options. She was deciding whether to cut me off or let me get to the point.

"You've got two minutes," she said, her voice clipped.

"It's about James," I started, my voice steadier now. This was the part that mattered.

The shift in her demeanor was immediate. "Is he okay?" she asked, concern cracking through her professional armor.

"Normally, no," I admitted, my jaw tightening. "But this morning was different. You made a difference, Savvy. He was himself again, even if just for a little while."

"Henry," she cut in, her voice sharpening like a blade. "If this is some manipulative ploy to drag me back into your family's mess..."

"It's not," I interrupted, sharper than I intended. I took a deep breath, forcing myself to stay calm. "This isn't about the family. It's about James. Please, he needs you."

There was a long stretch of silence. I could almost hear her pacing, the scrape of a chair, or the sound of footsteps muffled on the other end.

"Do you know what you're asking of me?" she said, her voice sharp and unsteady. "Do you even care what this has cost me? Henry, my career is..." She stopped herself, but I knew exactly what she was thinking, what she'd lost because of me.

"I didn't mean for any of this to happen," I said, guilt twisting in my chest. "I didn't want to hurt you, Savvy. Or your career."

"But you did," she snapped. "You always do. And now you want me to risk even more? For what?"

"For him," I said, my voice almost breaking. "For James. Because today ... today was the best day he's had in months, Savvy. You gave him that. And I want him to have more days like this, when he's himself again."

Her exhale was sharp, almost like a sardonic laugh, but there was no humor in it. "Well, I'm glad you got one good day, Henry, because I came home to find out your family is meddling in my life—again. Building inspections and last-minute Hail Marys from James? You can't stay out of my life, can you?"

"I know," I admitted, my jaw tightening. "My father is at it again. He's behind the inspector."

Her silence was heavy, loaded with anger and resignation.

"Of course he is," she said, her voice dripping with disdain. "Why wouldn't he be? God forbid Richard Kingston lets me live in peace."

"I'll fix it," I said quickly, my voice steady with a conviction I'm not sure I deserve. "I'll do whatever it takes to stop him. ... but don't let James spend his last days wondering what might have been. He needs you, Savvy. And whether or not you want to admit it, you know it."

She didn't reply immediately, but I heard her exhale—sharp and weary. "I told him I'd think about it," she said softly, almost like she was reminding herself.

"Thank you," I said, relief and guilt flooding through me all at once. "That's all I'm asking. Just ... don't wait too long. The good days are slipping away faster than we can hold onto them."

"Goodbye, Henry," she said, her voice sharper now, with a note of finality.

"Savvy, wait—"

The line went dead.

I dropped the phone into the passenger seat, the silence in the car suddenly deafening. For a long moment, I sat there, staring at the dashboard. I'd been able to fix things, smooth over the cracks, and keep the machine running. But this? This felt like trying to hold water in my hands. No matter what I did, it kept slipping through.

My phone buzzed again, pulling me back into reality.

MASON

Your father rescheduled the board meeting.
Tomorrow morning, 7 a.m.

Perfect. As if this day wasn't complicated enough.

I pressed Mason's name on the screen and waited as the line rang.

"Henry," he answered on the second ring, his voice curt. "I assume you got my message."

"Yeah," I said, rubbing a hand over my face. "Why the change? What's he up to now?"

"Your guess is as good as mine," Mason replied. "Something about ensuring everyone's priorities are ... aligned." He paused, letting the words hang in the air.

I exhaled sharply, frustration bubbling to the surface. "Mason, why are you even helping me? You know how this ends. You've seen it enough times to know my father doesn't lose."

There was a long stretch of silence on the other end, and I pictured Mason pacing wherever he was, debating whether to tell me the truth or feed me a line.

"Because someone has to," he said. "I can't fight him, but I can give you enough room to try."

For a moment, I was caught off guard. Mason had

115

always been loyal to my father—at least, that's what I'd thought. "You don't believe in him anymore, do you?"

"Let's say I know who Richard Kingston is," he replied, his voice sharper now. "And I know who you're trying to be. If you want to take him on, you'll need every advantage you can get."

I paused, unsure how to respond. Mason's words hit harder than I expected, and for the first time, I saw him as more than a shadow of my father's empire.

"Thank you," I said, the words feeling inadequate.

"Don't thank me yet," Mason replied. "Your father has a habit of turning advantages into liabilities. Be ready for tomorrow."

"I will," I promised, even as doubt coiled tight in my chest.

I started the car, the engine rumbling to life beneath me. The city lights stretched out ahead, glittering like a maze of dead ends. Tonight, all I could think about is the way Savvy's voice trembled when she said goodbye. And how, after everything, I still didn't know how to fix what I'd broken without breaking it all over again.

I gripped the steering wheel tightly, the doubt Mason planted in my mind growing roots. Tomorrow felt like a storm I couldn't fully prepare for, and the thought of facing my father with so much at stake made the air feel heavier in my chest.

But it wasn't the board meeting that had my thoughts tangled. It was her.

Savvy's goodbye kept replaying in my mind, soft and uneven, cutting deeper than I wanted to admit. I thought walking away once would protect her. I thought the distance would shield her from the fallout of my family's chaos. But I was wrong.

I glanced at my phone sitting in the console. My hand hovered over it, a thousand thoughts fighting for attention. For a moment, I just sat there.

Then I picked up the phone.

A long exhale escaped me as I typed her a message. My thumb hesitated for a fraction of a second before I pressed send.

The screen darkened as I set the phone back down and let my head rest against the seat. Tomorrow, everything could change—one way or another. For now, I could only drive forward and hope the pieces I'd set in motion didn't come crashing down.

CHAPTER FOURTEEN

Savvy

I headed up the narrow staircase to my apartment, my phone still buzzing in my hand. At my door, I paused, took a deep breath, and opened the latest message.

HENRY

Savvy, please don't shut me out. We need to talk.

I hesitated for a moment, my fingers hovering over the keyboard before typing back:

ME

You get one hour. Bookstore. Nine.

I pressed send, locking the door behind me. His reply came almost instantly.

HENRY

Thank you, Savvy. I'll be there.

Inside my apartment, I headed straight for the kitchen

and poured a generous glass of wine. The bookstore had been the right choice—quiet but still public. Not like this apartment, filled with personal photographs and morning coffee mugs. Even locked up, Mom's domain was like neutral ground. The shelves of books stood as sentinels, separating my personal life from whatever Henry was bringing to my door. Sure, the store had its own memories, but they were blurred by years of strangers' footsteps and the steady rhythm of business.

I took a long sip of wine and buried my face in my free hand. "You're playing with fire, Honeysucker," I told myself. "And you know exactly how this ends."

But as I stood to get ready, the feeling lingered—this time, the flames might just be worth the burn. At least here, surrounded by shelves of other people's stories, I could keep my walls up.

I set the glass down with a sigh, shaking my head to dispel the memories. This wasn't the time for nostalgia or second-guessing. My parents' livelihood was on the line, and if Henry thought he had something important to share, I needed to hear it.

———

FROM MY PERCH in the window seat, I saw him. My heart hammered against my ribs as I watched him approach the door. I'd spent countless evenings in this window seat, lost in other people's stories, but now my past was walking up to the door. I forced myself to wait until he was close before standing, my legs shakier than I wanted to admit.

The lock clicked beneath my fingers, loud in the empty store. As I pulled the door open, the night air rushed in, carrying his scent—sandalwood mingled with something unmistakably Henry—hitting me like a wave. Memories surged. The lazy Sundays spent together, stolen kisses within these walls, the safety of his arms around me. My fingers tightened on the edge of the door until they ached. *Keep it together, Savvy. You're not that naive girl anymore.*

"Savvy," he said, his voice low and inviting, and I cursed my traitorous pulse for responding to that familiar drawl.

"Henry," I said, keeping my voice steady. "Let's get on with it, okay?" A shadow of unease crossed his face, and despite everything, a pang of sympathy tightened in my chest. He'd dragged me into this chaos, but he was also helping me navigate it.

"Okay, then," he started, his fingers raking through his hair—a gesture I'd forgotten until now. "Thanks for agreeing to see me."

I shot him a skeptical look. "I'm here for one reason only —my family."

Henry's features hardened into a mix of resolve and understanding. "I understand, but there are matters you should be informed about—"

"Wait," I cut him off, hating the slight quiver in my voice that betrayed my tangled emotions. "I don't need a history lesson or excuses for what transpired years ago. Just explain how this predicament impacts River Bend Books."

He closed the gap between us by a step, and I steeled myself against the urge to back away from him, from our shared past and the possibility of a complicated future.

"This isn't as simple as you think," he replied, his voice steady but laced with quiet intensity. "There's history here, context you need to understand—"

"Backstory?" A dry chuckle escaped me, more sarcasm than bite this time. Our tangled history was nothing if not full of it. "Is that what we're calling our past? Backstory?

Quite the term from the man who disappeared without letting me have a say in my story."

Henry's jaw tightened, but he pressed on. "My father's interference in River Bend isn't new. Your family's business in the marina and bookstore have been in his sights for years. He's been methodically working to undermine your family, forcing me to make a choice. Your return gave him the momentum to move forward with his plans."

I tried to focus on his words, but my mind kept drifting. The familiar cadence of his voice and the way his brow furrowed when he was worried were all achingly familiar. *Stop it, Savvy. This isn't about you and him.*

"Mason told me about a board meeting scheduled for tomorrow, and I plan to be there," Henry announced, his voice laced with an undercurrent of urgency. "I'm certain my father's planning to use it as a launchpad to exploit River Bend."

My eyes widened, the sudden revelation momentarily throwing me off balance. "So, this is bigger than the bookstore?"

"Yes," he said. "I think my father plans to redevelop River Bend completely. If he gets his way, the marina, the main street, everything that gives this town its character— it'll all be gone. He'll flatten it, rebuild it into some lifeless corporate vision of progress, and leave nothing of what makes this place special."

I sat there, stunned into silence. His words pressed down on me, thickening the space between us with an unbearable weight. How could one person carry so much hatred? How could someone be so consumed by greed and power that they'd willingly destroy an entire town? To Richard Kingston, families, livelihoods, and memories were nothing more than collateral damage.

"How does someone become like that?" I murmured, almost to myself. "How do you hate so much that you're willing to destroy everything in your path to get what you want?"

Henry's gaze darkened, his jaw tightening. "It's not hate, Savvy. It's control. My father doesn't see people—he sees obstacles. And he removes them. Whether it's a business, a community, or..." He trailed off, his expression pained. "Or his own son."

The vulnerability in his voice caught me off guard, and for a moment, I saw the cracks in Henry's composed exterior. It wasn't shock or concern I was seeing—it was a deep, personal wound that had never fully healed.

I swallowed hard, my emotions threatening to spiral. "It's ... hard to comprehend," I said. "Your father's actions aren't about profit. They're personal. He's tearing this town apart, and for what? To prove he can?"

Henry nodded, his expression grim. "For Richard Kingston, power is everything. If he can crush River Bend, it'll solidify his legacy as someone unstoppable. He doesn't care how many lives he destroys in the process."

A laugh escaped me, though there was no humor in it. "And here I thought my life was complicated enough without adding 'saving the town' to my list of responsibilities."

Henry hesitated. "James has been helping me," he admitted. "He has connections in the city—inspectors, officials, people my father ignored because they didn't come with a price tag. He's made calls. If there's a way to stop my father, we'll find it."

I blinked at the mention of James tugging at a thread of memory. "Yes," I said, nodding. "My father told me James put a call into the city today. It's the only reason we're still open."

Henry exhaled, his relief palpable. "Good. That buys us time. James isn't done yet, either. He's reached out to some people with enough influence to push back. They'll stand with us if we can show them the evidence."

James Morrison's unwavering commitment to River Bend took root in my mind. This was the same man who had once sat in this bookstore, discussing poetry with my mother, and he was still battling for our town. I was struck by his understated resilience—a trait Henry must have inherited yet seldom revealed. This realization stirred a strange cocktail of emotions—an odd blend of hope and uncertainty.

A heavy silence settled between us. My eyes wandered over Henry's face, probing for answers I wasn't even sure he could provide. Then, almost involuntarily, I voiced the question that had haunted me since I delivered the breakup message.

"Henry," I began, my voice hesitant, "did you love her?"

His brow furrowed in confusion. "Who?"

"Caroline," I said, the name tasting foreign. "Were you in love with her?"

Henry's eyes widened, the question catching him off guard. He shook his head slowly, his gaze never leaving mine. "No," he said, his voice firm. "I didn't love her."

I blinked, surprised by the conviction in his tone. "Then why—"

"My father loved the idea of her," he said, his voice low, simmering with quiet anger. "And I was a pawn in a game I never wanted to play. That marriage wasn't about love, Savvy—it was a merger. A carefully calculated move to strengthen the Kingston empire." He let out a quiet, humorless laugh. "I spent my whole life feeling powerless in that family. Every decision, every move—it was all part of some grand Kingston plan. Until now."

His voice dropped lower, gaining an edge of steel I'd never heard before. "There's only ever been one woman I've loved, Savvy." His eyes locked onto mine with an intensity that made it impossible to look away. It was as though he was reaching into my soul, dragging the truth from a place I'd tried to keep buried. "I gave her up," he continued, his voice steady but laced with raw emotion. "Because I thought I was protecting her. Protecting you."

My breath hitched, his confession stealing the air from my lungs. The room seemed to fall away, leaving only him, his words, and the unbearable ache they carried. His eyes held mine with such intensity that I couldn't move, think, or breathe.

I opened my mouth to respond, to say something, anything—but the words wouldn't come. They lodged in my throat, blocked by the emotions raging inside me. Anger, confusion, longing, and something I refused to name churned together, leaving me defenseless against the truth shining in his eyes.

"Do you hear me, Savvy?" he asked, his voice dipping to a near-whisper, so low and intimate it felt like a confession meant only for me. "I thought I was doing the right thing. I thought walking away would save you. But every single day, I've regretted it."

The crack in his voice was small, but it was enough to break my composure. Emotion pulled tight inside me, the walls I'd built to keep him out crumbling around me.

His gaze grew intent, though it never wavered. "I know I don't deserve your forgiveness," he said, his voice thick with regret. "But if there's one thing I've learned, it's that I can't protect you by shutting you out. I won't make the same mistake again."

My heart thundered, the raw sincerity in his eyes pulling at something deep inside me, something I wasn't ready to confront. I wanted to be angry, push him away, and remind him of the hurt he'd caused. But his words, his voice, his expression, made that impossible.

I forced myself to speak, my voice unsteady with emotion. "Henry ... I don't even know what to say."

"You don't have to say anything," he said, stepping closer, the air between us humming with electricity, like the moment before a storm breaks. "Let me fight for you this time. For you, your family, and everything your father and mother built with so much sacrifice. I won't walk away again, Savvy. Not unless you tell me to."

The words hung between us, heavy with meaning and the possibility of something I couldn't yet define. My pulse raced as I searched his face, looking for any sign that this was a lie, a manipulation. But there was nothing—just Henry, standing before me, stripped of every pretense.

For the first time in years, I saw both the boy I'd loved and the man he'd become—flawed, broken, but undeniably real. And for one brief, terrifying moment, I allowed myself to imagine what it might mean to trust him again. Shaking off the thought, I straightened my shoulders and fixed my gaze on his. "I appreciate your honesty," I said, my voice steady despite the turmoil. "Finally. But Henry, this isn't about me or my family. This is about the entire town. If we're going to stop your father, we need more than promises. We need a plan."

Relief washed over his face, though it was quickly tempered by determination. "I'll give you everything I have, Savvy. Whatever it takes."

I nodded, my resolve hardening. "Then let's figure this out. Together."

Henry hesitated, his expression shifting. It wasn't relief or determination anymore—it was something deeper, almost vulnerable. "Savvy," he said, his voice catching, "I need you to know ... this won't be easy. And there are some things I'll have to do on my own."

I frowned. "What do you mean? If this concerns protecting my family, I have a right to be there. To fight for them."

Pain flashed across his face, and for a moment, I saw the cracks in his polished exterior. "You do," he said, his voice quiet but firm. "But tomorrow's board meeting isn't a fight you can be part of. They wouldn't let you past the door. It's shareholders and executives only, and if they see you there, it'll make everything worse. They'll shut me down before I even get started."

I stared at him, a mix of frustration and helplessness bubbling to the surface. "So, what am I supposed to do? Sit back and wait while you face them alone?"

Henry stepped closer, his gaze steady and unwavering. "You won't just be waiting. I'll keep you in the loop every step of the way. But this part? This part has to be me." He paused, his voice lowering. "Savvy, I promise—I won't lock you out of this. Never again. But if we're going to win, I need to play this right."

He wasn't brushing me aside or underestimating me. He was laying out the reality of the situation, painful as it was.

"Fine," I said after a long pause, the word tasting sour in my mouth. "But if you think for one second that I'll let you keep me in the dark, you're dead wrong. The moment you leave that meeting, I want to know everything."

"Deal." A hint of relief crossed his face, but his voice remained resolute. "This isn't just my fight, Savvy. It's ours."

Our fight. The words lingered in the air, foreign and strangely comforting at the same time. I wanted to push him away, to hold on to the anger that had shielded me for so long, but the cracks in my defenses were widening. Henry Kingston had a way of doing that—slipping past my walls, leaving me exposed to emotions I didn't want to feel.

I took a deep breath, crossing my arms to steady myself. "And after the board meeting? What then?"

"Then we regroup," he said, his voice steady. "We figure out our next move. My father won't go down without a war."

"Good," I said, my chin lifting defiantly. "Because I'm not afraid of a fight."

For a moment, Henry looked at me, something unreadable in his eyes. "I know," he said. "You've never been afraid of anything. That's one thing I've admired about you."

I looked away, the intensity in his voice too much to bear. The room seemed to close in around me, the pressure of our conversation mounting with each passing second. "You'd better not let me down, Henry," I said, my voice barely more than a whisper. "Because if you do..."

"I won't," he interrupted, his eyes never leaving mine. "Not this time."

The sincerity in his voice sent a shiver down my spine, but I forced myself to stay composed. I couldn't afford to let hope creep in—not yet. Not when so much was still uncertain.

Henry stepped back, his movements deliberate. "I should go," he said, glancing at the clock on the wall. "It's late, and you have enough to deal with without me standing here making things harder."

I didn't respond, my throat too tight to speak. Instead, I watched as he moved toward the door, his hand hesitating on the knob.

"Savvy," he said, turning back to face me. "No matter what happens tomorrow, I want you to know ... I'm not walking away again. I'll see this through—for you, your family, and River Bend. And after that, well..." He paused. "After that, I'll leave it up to you."

My heart twisted, the vulnerability in his words cutting deeper than I wanted to admit. I nodded, my emotions too tangled to form a coherent response.

Henry opened the door, the cool night air rushing in as he stepped outside. For a moment, he lingered on the threshold as if waiting for me to say something, anything, to stop him. But I stayed silent, rooted in place, until he disappeared into the shadows.

I turned back to the quiet of the bookstore, the rows of books suddenly feeling like a refuge and a cage all at once. Mom's organized world surrounded me—the neat stack of invoices on her counter, the perfectly aligned bestseller display, everything in its proper place. Everything except me, standing here with my heart thundering in my chest.

I was drawn to the window, my fingers brushing the cool glass as I stared into the empty street.

"Don't mess this up, Henry," I whispered to the night. "Please, don't screw this up."

CHAPTER FIFTEEN

Henry

I drew a deep breath, bracing myself before pushing open the heavy oak doors to the boardroom. The tension inside was almost palpable, the air charged with the gravity of decisions that could alter River Bend's future. As I stepped in, my gaze immediately landed on my father at the head of the table—Richard Kingston III, the embodiment of corporate dominance, his tailored suit immaculate, his silver hair precisely styled. He was mid-sentence, but the words died on his lips the moment he saw me.

"Henry," he said, recovering quickly. "I wasn't expecting you today."

The room fell silent, a dozen pairs of eyes turning toward me. I kept my expression steady, feigning ease. "Wouldn't miss it for the world, Dad."

As I took a seat, I caught the subtle tightening of his jaw. He was pissed, but he wouldn't make a scene. Not here, not now, with all these witnesses. I nodded at a few familiar faces around the table. Some seemed curious, others skeptical. I wondered how many of them my father had won over.

Dad cleared his throat, reclaiming the room's attention. "As I was saying, gentlemen, our vision for River Bend is nothing short of transformative."

I listened as he launched into his pitch, his voice smooth as silk, painting a picture of progress and prosperity. But all I could see was the destruction of everything that made the town special. The local businesses pushed out, replaced by chain stores and overpriced condos. The marina where I spent my summers turned into a sterile yacht club with waterfront mansions.

My hands clenched under the table as I thought of Savvy, of her family's bookstore. Of all the people who called River Bend home, blissfully unaware of the storm headed their way.

"This project will bring River Bend into the 21st century," my father continued, his eyes gleaming with barely contained triumph. "We're not just developing property. We're creating a legacy."

A legacy built on lies and manipulation, I thought. But I forced myself to stay calm, to listen. I needed to know exactly what we were up against if I had any hope of stopping this.

As Richard droned on about projected profits and property values, my mind drifted to my mother. What would she think of all this? She loved River Bend as much as I did, but she was too afraid to stand up to my father. I wondered if she even knew the full extent of his plans.

River Bend wasn't just another town—it was a place where people looked out for each other, where a handshake still meant something, and where life moved at a pace that let you breathe. There was an honesty to it, a simplicity that felt like stepping back into a time when the world wasn't so complicated. It was the kind of town where neighbors showed up unannounced with casseroles when you were sick and where the waitress at the diner knew your order by heart. There weren't any hidden agendas, no fine print. Just real people living real lives.

And my father wanted to bulldoze it all in favor of something shinier, something that would never have the heart of the place it replaced.

"Questions?" Richard's voice snapped me back to attention. He was looking around the room, his gaze skipping me as if I wasn't even there.

I cleared my throat. "Actually, I have a few concerns about the impact on local businesses."

The room stilled, and I could feel every stare pressing in on me. My father's eyes narrowed, but his voice remained perfectly controlled. "I'm sure we can discuss that privately, Henry. This isn't really the time or place."

But I wasn't backing down. Not this time. "I think it's exactly the time and place, Dad. If we're going to reshape River Bend, shouldn't we consider all perspectives?"

The gravity of the moment settled over me, and I steadied myself. This wasn't just about a development project anymore. It was about the heart of a city. It was about Savvy. And I'd be damned if I let it slip away without a fight.

I stood abruptly, my chair scraping against the polished floor. My heart pounded so hard I swore the board members could hear it, but I forced my voice to remain steady.

"I'm sorry, but I can't sit here and listen to this without speaking up." I paused, doubt gnawing at my insides. What if I was wrong? What if I was making a fool of myself?

But then I thought of Savvy's face, of the bookstore

where we shared our first kiss, of the marina where her family's dreams were anchored. A rush of adrenaline flooded my system, and suddenly, I knew I had to do this.

"Progress is a double-edged sword," I began, my voice steady despite the turmoil inside me. "It can build cities, create opportunities, but it can also destroy lives." I pictured River Bend Books, the soul of the town, teetering on the brink of extinction because of my father's plans. "He's been playing a dangerous game—manipulating property values and undermining local businesses to force sales and swell his own coffers."

My words hung heavy in the room as I turned to Caroline's father. A silent plea passed from me to him—an unspoken appeal to look beyond corporate gains and power shifts, to recognize the human toll of this venture.

"This isn't merely about River Bend," I added quietly, the gravity of my next words pressing against my ribs like a vice. "It reaches into our personal lives too." My gaze locked onto his, the intensity between us almost something I could reach out and hold.

Dad's dismissive smirk sliced through me like a serrated knife. "Ah, the wayward heir graces us with his presence," he sneered. "What motivates your visit today, Henry? Another one of your noble yet doomed endeavors?"

He paused for dramatic effect, his voice dripping with derision. "Like that virtual reality fitness app you tried to get off the ground during your first year at college?"

His words hit their mark, and I could feel my cheeks flush with embarrassment and indignation. Of course, he would dredge up that old failure. I took a moment to steady my breath, reminding myself of the reason I was here.

"This isn't about me, Dad," I said, proud of how steady my voice sounded. "It's about the people of River Bend."

I reached into my briefcase, extracting an inspection report for River Bend Books. "There's never been a problem with this property until your company showed interest in buying it." I laid the report on the table for all to see. "Are we really going to acquire River Bend by manipulating data and bribing inspectors to create situations where tenants can't afford to stay? Is that what we're calling progress now?"

Martha Reinhardt, head of the ethics committee, snatched up the papers, her eyes widening as she scanned the contents. To my left, Gerald Peterson moved uncomfortably in his seat.

"These are serious allegations," Martha said, her voice tight. "If true, they warrant a full investigation."

I could feel the room's energy shifting. Some board members leaned in, clearly intrigued. Others eyed the exit, as if proximity to this scandal might be contagious.

"We can't move forward with a vote until we know the full story," I pressed. "River Bend isn't a collection of properties to be bought and sold. It's a community. People's lives and livelihoods are at stake."

While I argued my point, visions of Savvy danced in my thoughts. I wasn't fighting for a town. I was fighting for a future I thought I'd lost.

My father's eyes narrowed, and I braced myself for whatever came next. The silence between us stretched, and for a moment, I was that little boy again—desperate for approval, afraid of letting him down.

But I wasn't that boy anymore. And River Bend needed me to be stronger than that.

As the pressure in the room peaked, my gaze drifted to Mason. He sat at the far end of the table, his face carefully neutral. But the set of his shoulders, the way his fingers drummed an irregular rhythm against the polished mahogany, told a different story.

Mason and I went way back to a time when his father was still around, working as my father's right-hand man. He locked gazes with me across the room, and I detected a fleeting glimmer of ... something in his eyes. Compassion? Understanding? It vanished before I could fully grasp it, but he offered an almost unnoticed nod of acknowledgment.

"Mr. Kingston," Mason said, his voice low but carrying. "Perhaps we should consider a brief recess to review these accusations?"

My father's head whipped around, surprise flashing across his face before he schooled his features. "I hardly think that's necessary, Mason. Henry's ... creative interpretation of events hardly warrants—"

"With all due respect, sir," Mason cut in, and I had to bite back a grin at the barely veiled insolence in his voice, "I believe it's our fiduciary duty to investigate any potential impropriety."

As the board members started their hushed conversations, my thoughts drifted back to those carefree summer days spent by the Kingston pool, Mason and I, awkward adolescents, envisioning our futures while our fathers discussed business matters over cocktails. I recalled vividly the day Mason's father was no longer there, the grief in his eyes as he cleared out his dad's office.

I had always thought Mason bore a grudge against me, blaming his father's untimely death on the incessant demands of serving the Kingston clan. But after graduation, he stepped into his father's shoes as if it were all part of an orchestrated plan. Observing him now, noticing the careful way he carried himself... Maybe I'd been misjudging him all along.

"Fair enough," my father conceded grudgingly, though his expression remained distant. "We'll reconvene in an hour. That should be enough time to address these ... issues."

The board members slowly rose from their seats, murmuring among themselves as they drifted out for the break. I caught Mason's eye before he exited. This time, a trace of something—amusement, maybe approval—tugged at the corners of his mouth. It seemed I might have found an unexpected ally in this fight.

When the hour was up, the room filled again, the air heavy with unspoken decisions. The murmur of side conversations quieted as the board members settled into their seats, their focus shifting to the table. Deliberations resumed, the low hum of whispers threading an undercurrent of unease. I scanned their faces, searching for any hint of where they stood. Mrs. Hawthorne's furrowed brow, Mr. Carlson's incessant pen-tapping, and the way Ms. Rodriguez's gaze moved between my father and me—each movement was a piece of a high-stakes puzzle waiting to be solved.

"This is ridiculous," my father muttered, loud enough for me to hear. "A waste of valuable time."

I held back a response, aware that my silence was the most potent weapon I possessed at that moment. Instead, I let my eyes wander to the window, where the distant cityscape twinkled with countless lights. New York City. Miles away from River Bend. The reason I was here, gambling it all.

After what seemed like an eternity, the chairman cleared his throat. "Considering the concerns raised, we've delayed the vote for two weeks. This will give us time to investigate the allegations thoroughly."

Relief flooded through me, but I kept my expression neutral. It wasn't a victory, not yet. But it was a start.

As the boardroom emptied, my father's gaze bore into me. He didn't need to speak—the tight set of his jaw said it all. I'd thrown down the gauntlet, and it was only a matter of time before he crafted his counterattack.

I made my way out of the building, scrolling to Savvy's name on my phone. My fingers hovered for a moment before I hit *dial*.

"Henry?"

"Yeah." I replied. "The meeting has ended. There's a lot we need to discuss."

Without missing a beat, she told me, "I'm on my way to the Madison Center to see James." A warm ripple spread through me at her words.

"When you get there, stay put," I said. "I'm on my way."

CHAPTER SIXTEEN

Savvy

Sunlight streamed through the tall windows, catching on the polished floors as I entered Madison Center. I stopped by the reception desk to sign in and pick up my visitor pass.

The nurse behind the counter looked up, her expression warm and welcoming. "Oh, you're back! James was practically glowing after your visit yesterday. It's been a while since we've seen him so energized."

Her words sparked a touch of warmth, a reassurance that my visit had mattered. "Good to know," I said, sliding the pass over my head. "I'll do my best not to wear him out this time."

I clutched my battered copy of *Jane Eyre* tighter as I walked down the hall. Yesterday, when James asked me to return, I hadn't promised anything. "Not for Henry," he'd said, his sharp eyes piercing me. "For me."

At the time, I'd nodded, unsure if I could face this place —or him—again.

But now I was here, my heart buzzing with nerves as I reached his door.

James was in his usual spot by the window, his face turned toward the golden autumn light filtering through the trees outside. His head tilted at the sound of my footsteps, and a smile spread across his weathered features when he saw me.

"Ah, Savannah," he greeted, his voice warm but faintly strained. "I knew you'd come."

I closed the door behind me and stepped toward the chair beside him. "Hi, James."

His gaze flicked to the book in my hands, his lips twitching into a grin. "And with *Jane Eyre*, no less. Fitting, don't you think, considering the Honeysucker-Kingston saga?"

I let out a quiet laugh, despite myself. "It seemed appropriate."

James chuckled and gestured for me to sit. "Good. Let's argue about Rochester while I still have the energy."

I took the seat beside him, setting the book on my lap. "I thought you might have more important things on your mind today."

"Important things, yes." He reached for my hand, his grip lighter than it had been yesterday. "Like reminding you how stubborn you are. Though I suppose that's why you'll succeed where I failed."

His words pulled me up short. "James, you've never—"

"I have," he interrupted gently. "More times than I care to admit. For Henry's sake, I should have stood up to Richard years ago. For your sake. But I didn't. And I regret it every day."

My throat tightened as I studied his face, the lines of his years gentled by the afternoon light. "You've done more for me than anyone in that family ever has. You don't owe me anything."

His hand squeezed mine. "You're wrong, Savannah. I owe you—and Henry—more than I could ever repay. That's why I need you to be strong. To fight for what's right. For River Bend. And..." He paused, his gaze turning thoughtful. "And maybe for him, too, if he proves he's worth it."

I opened my mouth, but before I could speak, the door creaked open behind me.

Henry's presence filled the room before he even stepped inside. My breath caught as I turned to see him, his broad shoulders framed by the doorway. His eyes immediately found mine, the flicker of surprise quickly replaced by something deeper.

"Grandfather," Henry greeted, his voice steady. "Savvy."

"Henry," I replied, my voice more guarded.

James lit up at the sight of him. "Henry. Don't stand there looking like you've been caught skipping church."

Henry sat down across from me. His face was etched with a calm that didn't quite match the strain in the room. The air grew thick with things unsaid and the pull of too much history.

James didn't seem to notice, or perhaps he ignored it. "Now that we're all here," he began, "let me tell you what I've admired about places like River Bend."

Henry and I both glanced at him, caught off guard by the shift in conversation.

"It's not just the charm," James continued, his voice soft but steady. "It's the people. Small towns take care of their own. They show up when it matters."

I nodded, emotion pressing against my ribs.

"You don't see that in cities like New York," James went

on, his gaze drifting out the window. "People get so caught up in their own ambition that they forget what matters. But in a place like River Bend, you notice when someone's hurting. You look out for each other."

He turned his attention to Henry, his expression growing more serious. "That's what I should've done more of. Look out for the people who matter instead of letting your father dictate the rules. Don't make that same mistake, Henry."

Henry's jaw tightened, but he leaned forward, his voice quieter than usual. "You've looked out for me, Grandfather."

"When I could," James admitted. "But I didn't do enough. Not for you. Not for Savannah."

His gaze shifted between us, his words landing with quiet finality.

Henry stood and touched his shoulder when James's head dipped, his energy fading. "We should let him rest."

Before we left, James regained a moment of clarity. His frail hands caught ours, his grip weak but purposeful. "Take care of each other," he murmured.

The drive back to River Bend was silent, both of us lost in thought. When Henry slowed the car on Main Street, he glanced at me. "Do you want to take a walk?"

I hesitated for only a moment before nodding. "Okay."

The town was calm, its quiet streets glowing in the soft light of the early sun. As we walked, we stopped to chat with familiar faces—Mrs. Patterson was setting up the post office display, and Old Mr. Dixon was arranging the crates outside The Weathered Barn.

"We need to warn them," I said softly after Mrs. Patterson bustled inside with her packages.

Henry nodded. "Yes, they need to know what's coming.

That no matter what they hear about inspections or offers to sell, they have to hold the line."

We moved from one person to the next, sharing what we knew about Richard Kingston's looming plans. Henry's voice was measured and steady, but it carried an undercurrent of urgency that struck a chord with everyone we spoke to.

"Don't sell," he urged Mrs. Patterson. "No matter what you're offered, regardless of what you hear about the state of your building. We'll ensure you understand your property's true value and get you the resources to protect it."

Mrs. Patterson's sharp eyes narrowed as understanding dawned. "I'll spread the word," she promised. "Everyone will know by sundown that we're standing together."

I didn't doubt her. Mrs. Patterson could move news faster than the internet in River Bend, and right now, that network could be our strongest defense.

As we continued our walk in the late morning sun, Henry's presence beside me felt steady, more like a lifeline than a burden. His focus on protecting the community reminded me of the boy I once loved, who fought for what was right, no matter the cost.

When we reached my apartment, I paused at the door, struck by how naturally we'd fallen back into sync today.

"Do you want to come in for coffee?" The words tumbled out before I could stop them. "We need to gather resources before your father makes his move."

Henry's eyebrows lifted, a look of approval playing across his face. "I'd like that. I've got all day, and I have some contacts we should call."

The hours flew by in a whirlwind of productivity. Henry worked with his corporate contacts while I contacted local property owners. My coffee table became command central, covered in property assessments and legal documents. Henry's laptop chimed with incoming emails as responses from law firms trickled in.

"Martinez & Associates is in," Henry announced around two o'clock, running a hand through his disheveled hair. "Pro bono representation for any resident facing pressure tactics."

I looked up from my stack of papers, grinning. "That's three firms now. And I've got two independent inspectors willing to do fair market assessments at reduced rates."

Henry exhaled, shaking his head in disbelief. "It's not just about business for them. My father's burned a lot of bridges over the years—strong-arming locals, undercutting contracts, making it impossible for small firms to compete. They've been waiting for a chance to push back."

When our stomachs started growling, Henry ordered pizza. We ate straight from the box, comparing notes between bites. His tie had long since been discarded, sleeves rolled up to his elbows as he paced, talking to another contact. I couldn't help but notice how the muscles in his forearms flexed as he gestured.

The sun was setting when Henry ended his last call. "That's five law firms total," he said, dropping onto the couch beside me. "And a promise from my old professor to review any contracts that come through."

I stared at our day's work spread across the coffee table, overwhelmed by what we'd accomplished. "We're doing this," I breathed. "We're fighting back."

"We are," Henry said. When I turned to look at him, I found his face inches from mine.

The air between was filled with something more than victory. We'd been brushing past each other all day, sharing looks, working in perfect sync. Now, with no more calls to make or emails to send, I couldn't ignore the electricity anymore.

"Savvy," Henry breathed, his hand coming to rest on my knee. The warmth of his touch sent shivers up my spine.

I knew I should focus on our work and the community counting on us. But as Henry leaned in, his lips inches from mine, all my boundaries disintegrated.

Our lips met in an achingly familiar and thrillingly new kiss. It was soft at first, tentative, but quickly deepened into something more urgent. Years of pent-up longing and regret poured into that kiss, mingled now with the pride and passion of our shared mission.

When we broke apart, breathless, my mind spun with conflicting emotions. The floodgates had opened, and I was drowning in everything I'd tried to forget. Was this brilliant or completely reckless? My brain screamed that we had too much at stake, that mixing business with pleasure could jeopardize everything we'd worked for today. My heart whispered of second chances and destined timing. And my body ... my body wanted him closer.

"Stay," I heard myself whisper. The word emerged from some deep place I hadn't even known was ruling my actions.

Henry's answer was another searing kiss, his hands tangling in my hair as he pulled me closer. Warning bells rang distantly in my mind, but the thunder of my pulse drowned them out, as did the electric feeling of his fingers against my scalp and the intoxicating familiarity of his cologne.

As we rose from the couch, papers scattered to the floor, I couldn't tell if this was the smartest or stupidest decision I'd ever made. But in that moment, with Henry's lips trailing fire down my neck, I realized I didn't care. Tomorrow could worry about itself.

We stumbled toward the bedroom, leaving a trail of discarded clothing in our wake. Each touch and each kiss obliterated another rational thought until nothing was left but sensation and need. And when Henry whispered my name against my skin, I surrendered completely to whatever force—logic, love, or pure desire—had brought us to this moment. Right or wrong, there was no turning back now.

CHAPTER SEVENTEEN

Henry

The word "stay" echoed in my mind as I followed Savvy down the hallway, my heart thundering against my ribs. The familiar scent of her shampoo drifted back to me—vanilla and something uniquely her—awakening memories I'd spent years trying to suppress.

Her fingers laced through mine as she led me toward her bedroom, and the slight tremor in her hand didn't go unnoticed. It mirrored my uncertainty and my desperate need to get this right. After everything I'd done wrong, everything I'd broken between us, this moment was as precarious as walking on glass.

The moonlight filtering through her bedroom window painted silver streaks across her face as she turned to me. For a heartbeat, we stood there, suspended between what we'd been and what we could become. Her eyes carried the same mix of desire and fear that churned in my chest.

"Savvy," I breathed, reaching up to trace my thumb along her jaw. "If you want to stop—"

She silenced me with another kiss, deeper and more urgent than before. Her fingers traced across my bare chest, clutching my shoulders as if afraid I might disappear. The thought sent a sharp pain through me. Of course, she'd fear that—wasn't I the one who'd vanished before?

I wanted to tell her so many things—how I'd never stopped loving her, how leaving her had been like carving out my heart. But words felt too small, too fragile to carry the weight of our history. So instead, I let my touch speak, pouring everything I couldn't say into the way my hands found hers.

My hands slid down her sides, memorizing every curve like a drowning man finding shore. The silk of her blouse whispered beneath my touch as I traced the path I remembered so well, but I needed more—needed to feel her skin against mine.

"Let me," I murmured against her neck when her fingers fumbled with my buttons. "Let me look at you."

She nodded, a shiver passing through her as I unbuttoned her blouse. Each new inch of skin revealed was a revelation—the hollow of her throat, the delicate lines of her collarbones, that perfect freckle that had haunted my dreams for five years.

"You kept me awake at night," I confessed, pressing my lips to that beloved mark. "Wondering if you still tasted the same." My tongue traced the spot, drawing a gasp from her lips. "If you'd still make that sound when I..."

Her back arched as I found that sensitive place where her neck met her shoulder, the one that drove her wild.

"Henry," she breathed, her fingers digging into my arms.

I stepped forward, guiding her backward until her calves met the edge of her bed. She sank down onto the mattress, drawing me with her, our bodies finding that familiar dance even after all these years. The springs creaked softly as I followed her down, bracing myself above her. Her hair fanned out across the pale sheets like spilled ink in the moonlight, and for a moment, I could barely breathe at the sight of her.

She was laid out before me in the moonlight, more beautiful than I remembered, with all soft curves and subtle strength. Every inch of her skin called to me, begging to be touched, explored, remembered all over again.

"You're staring," she whispered, a touch of self-consciousness in her voice.

"Can't help it." I traced the curve of her breast with reverent fingers. "You're perfect."

Her laugh caught on a moan as I replaced my fingers with my mouth. I remembered exactly how she liked to be touched—soft kisses trailing lower, teeth grazing enough to make her gasp. Her hands tangled in my hair as I worked my way down her body, tasting and teasing until she was writhing beneath me.

"Please," she begged, her voice breaking on the word.

But I wasn't done worshipping her yet. I wanted—needed—to drive her as crazy as she'd made me these past days. My tongue traced patterns on her inner thigh, so close to where she wanted me, but not quite there.

"Henry," she pleaded, her hips rising. "Don't tease."

The rest of her plea was lost in a gasp as I savored her, my tongue moving in slow, deliberate strokes that had her unraveling beneath me.

I knew her body—remembered exactly how to touch her to make her come undone. But tonight, I wanted to take my time and make her feel everything I couldn't say with words.

I brought her to the edge slowly, relentlessly, then

pulled back as she tensed. Her frustrated whimper made me smile against her thigh.

"You're terrible," she gasped, tugging at my hair.

"Just thorough," I murmured, pressing open-mouthed kisses along her inner thigh. "We have five years to make up for."

I started again, slower this time, alternating between soft licks and firmer pressure until she was arching off the bed. But before she could fall over the edge, I pulled back again.

"Henry," she groaned, her voice hoarse with need. "Please..."

"Please, what?" I asked, my breath hot against her sensitive skin.

Her answer was lost in another moan as I resumed my attention, adding a finger, then two, curling them the way she used to love. Her thighs clenched around me, her breathing growing ragged.

This time, when she got close, I didn't stop. I took her higher and higher until she shattered, crying out. The sound of it—raw and desperate—nearly broke my control.

I kissed my way back up her body as she caught her breath, savoring the salt of her skin and the way she shivered at each touch. When I reached her mouth, she pulled me into a deep kiss.

"My turn," she whispered against my mouth, pushing me onto my back. Her hands traced down my chest, nails scraping lightly in a way that made me shudder. But when she tried to move lower, I caught her wrist.

"Not yet," I said, my voice rough. "I'm not done with you."

I rolled her beneath me again, capturing her protests with a kiss. My hands found hers, pinning them gently above her head as I explored her neck, her breasts, and every inch of skin I could reach. She writhed against me, seeking friction, but I held back.

"You're killing me," she gasped as I lavished attention on her breasts, alternating between gentle and demanding touches until she was arching into my mouth.

"You feel incredible," I murmured against her skin. "So perfect." I released her hands to trail my fingers down her stomach, feeling the muscles quiver beneath my touch. "I've dreamed about this. About making you fall apart again and again."

When I slipped my fingers between her legs once more, she was desperate for release. I worked her slowly, deliberately, watching her face as she climbed higher. Before she peaked, I withdrew again.

"No," she moaned, her eyes flying open. "Henry, please..."

"Not yet," I whispered, reaching for my wallet on the nightstand. My hands shook as I retrieved the condom, but Savvy's touch steadied me as she helped roll it on.

When I pushed into her, we both gasped, the sensation knocking the breath from my lungs. I had to pause, overwhelmed by how perfectly we fit together.

"Move," she begged, her legs wrapping around my waist.

I moved slowly at first, savoring each moment of connection. My forehead pressed to hers, breathing her in as our eyes locked. Everything I couldn't say poured into each tender touch—every regret, every promise, every moment I'd missed her.

"You're everything," I whispered, meaning it with every fiber of my being. Her hands traced patterns on my back as we found our rhythm together, rediscovering the perfect synchronization we'd once known so well.

"Henry," she gasped, her voice cracking. The sound of it —raw and unguarded—nearly undid me. Years of longing, regret, and missing her all came crashing into this moment of reconnection.

When she came apart beneath me, I followed right after, overwhelmed by the intensity of it all. For several heartbeats, we just held each other.

I gathered her close, pressing soft kisses to her temple, her cheeks, anywhere I could reach. She curled into me the way she used to, fitting perfectly against my side.

"Stay," she whispered against my chest, vulnerability threading through her voice.

I tightened my arms around her. "You couldn't drag me away if you tried," I murmured into her hair. "This is our beginning. The start of forever." She stiffened against me, and my heart stuttered.

"Henry..." She took a shaky breath. "Can we just ... take it one day at a time?"

The hesitation in her voice cut deep, but I understood. I'd earned her wariness, her reluctance to trust in me forever again. "Of course," I said, pressing a kiss to her temple. "Whatever you need."

She relaxed, curling back into me. Soon, her breathing evened out, but sleep eluded me. I lay awake, watching moonlight paint shadows across her peaceful face, wondering if she regretted our actions.

I didn't. I couldn't. Having her in my arms again was like coming home after years of wandering. The woman beside me wasn't the girl I'd left behind. She was stronger, more complex, and somehow even more beautiful for having been broken and rebuilt.

Tomorrow would bring its own challenges. We still had my father to face, years of hurt to heal, trust to rebuild. She might need time—might always keep one foot ready to run —but I would spend every day proving myself worthy of her trust.

Because Savvy Honeysucker wasn't just the woman I loved—she was everything. And even if she weren't ready to believe in forever, I would wait. I would show her, day by day, that this time was different.

This time, I was here to stay.

CHAPTER EIGHTEEN

Savvy

Dawn crept through my bedroom window, painting everything in shades of rose and gold, including Henry Kingston's sleeping form beside me.

Oh god. Oh god, oh god, oh god.

I eased out of bed, careful not to wake him, and grabbed my phone from the nightstand. My hands shook as I typed:

ME

911. Timeless Treats. NOW.

Ivy responded instantly:

OMG, what happened??

MADDY

On my way. Do we need weapons?

ME

Just caffeine and carbs. Code Henry.

MADDY

CODE HENRY??? Be there in 10.

IVY

I'll be there in 5.

I glanced back at Henry, his face peaceful in sleep, dark lashes fanning against his cheeks. He looked younger like this, like the boy who used to sneak up to my window with coffee and dreams. My heart ached at the memory.

Focus, Savvy.

I dressed quickly and silently, years of practice sneaking around my parents' bookstore coming in handy. At my desk, I hesitated before scribbling a note:

Had to run out. Used the last K-Cup, so you'll have to go downstairs if you want coffee.
Sav

Short. Professional. Nothing like the emotional mess churning inside me.

Would I regret this note the way I'd regretted letting him stay? Or would I regret not writing something more? Something that acknowledged how he'd whispered *"forever"* against my skin, the way I'd wanted desperately to believe him?

I dressed and crept down the back stairs, praying they wouldn't creak and alert my mother. The last thing I needed was to explain why I was sneaking out of my apartment at dawn.

I stepped onto the sidewalk, exhaling in relief—until I rounded the corner and nearly collided with my mother.

She stood outside, a spray bottle in one hand, a squeegee in the other, washing the bookstore's front windows.

Her gaze flicked from my messy hair to my wrinkled clothes, then past me to Henry Kingston's very distinctive, very *still parked* car.

She arched an eyebrow. "Going somewhere?"

"Uh... meeting the girls for breakfast," I blurted out, smoothing a hand over my hair like that would somehow erase the evidence.

Mom hummed, giving the window an exaggerated swipe. "Mmm hmm. And would this early morning *break-fast meeting* have anything to do with Henry Kingston still being upstairs?"

I opened my mouth, but nothing resembling an actual excuse came out.

She just smiled. "Thought so."

Heat flooded my cheeks. "Mom—"

"I'm just saying," she continued, "maybe it's time to consider an apartment that isn't connected to your mother's workplace."

"Trust me," I muttered, "that thought has crossed my mind."

I started to walk away, then hesitated. "Mom?"

She didn't even look up from her window washing. "Don't worry, honey. I won't tell your father. *Yet.*"

Perfect. Just perfect.

I turned onto Main Street, walking fast, as if I could outpace the growing list of complications in my life. Mrs. Patterson was already out with her tiny dog, and the perceptive glance she shot me suggested today's neighborhood watch update would be anything but dull.

Timeless Treats glowed like a beacon ahead, the smell of fresh pastries and coffee drawing me in. I could see through the window that Ivy and Maddy had claimed our usual corner booth. Karen, the owner, was heading their way with what looked like emergency-sized portions of everything.

The bell chimed as I pushed through the door, and my friends' heads snapped up.

"Spill," Ivy demanded the moment I slid into the booth. "Every. Single. Detail."

"Starting with why you look like you've been thoroughly —" Maddy began.

"Don't finish that sentence." I grabbed a chocolate croissant, needing sugar before this conversation. "I might have done something stupid."

"Define stupid," Maddy said, sliding a massive latte toward me.

I took a fortifying sip. "I may have slept with Henry."

"May have?" Ivy's eyebrows shot up.

"Okay, fine. Did. Definitely did." I buried my face in my hands. "Multiple times."

"Multiple!" Maddy crowed, drawing looks from other early-morning customers. She lowered her voice. "Details. Now."

"It was..." I searched for words that wouldn't sound downright pathetic. "Perfect. Intense. Everything I remembered and somehow more." The croissant crumbled in my nervous fingers. "And probably a horrible mistake."

"Why?" Ivy asked softly. "If it was so perfect?"

"Because it was amazing. He was amazing. Sweet and passionate and..." I swallowed hard. "He said it was forever."

"And that's bad?" Maddy looked confused.

"It's terrifying! Five years ago, he walked away without a word. Now he's talking about forever?" I grabbed another croissant. "What if I let myself believe him and he disappears again?"

"Or," Ivy said, "what if he means it?"

"God," Maddy sighed dreamily, "I can't remember the last time I had sex that warranted this level of panic."

"Right?" Ivy agreed. "My last date spent twenty minutes talking about his cryptocurrency investments."

"At least yours didn't describe his relationship with his mother as 'very close' while showing you pictures of their matching Christmas sweaters," Maddy countered.

Despite myself, I laughed. "You two aren't helping."

"We are," Ivy said. "We're reminding you that good men —especially good men who know exactly how to make you scream their name—"

"I never said anything about screaming!"

"Your face says it all, honey." She smirked. "The point is, good men are rare. And when one shows up, ready to fight for you, maybe don't run away because you're scared."

"I'm not running," I protested. "I'm being cautious."

"You're hiding in a bakery at dawn," Maddy pointed out. "That's the definition of running."

"I'm not hiding," I insisted, reaching for my third pastry. "I'm ... strategizing."

"With carbs?" Maddy grinned.

"They're brain food." I licked chocolate from my fingers. "And I need all the help I can get right now."

"Okay." Ivy leaned forward, all business. "Let's break this down. The sex was clearly amazing—"

"Mind-blowing," I admitted.

"Obviously. Your hair's still doing that post-sex thing it does."

I frantically patted my head. "What thing?"

"That 'I've been thoroughly ravished' waves thing," Maddy supplied helpfully. "Very romance novel heroine."

"I hate you both."

"No, you don't." Ivy pushed another latte toward me. "Now, besides the clearly epic sex, what else happened?"

I traced the rim of my cup, remembering. "He was ... different. More open. He told me about fighting his father at the board meeting and about trying to protect River Bend. About wanting to make things right."

"That sounds promising," Maddy said.

"And terrifying." I slumped back. "What if I trust him again and it all falls apart? What if—"

"What if you spend the rest of your life wondering what might have been?" Ivy cut in.

"Look, we were there five years ago. We watched you piece yourself back together. But Sav, maybe it's time to stop running the breakup business and let yourself believe in happy endings again."

"Says the professional bridesmaid," I muttered.

"Exactly! I see true love every day. And the way Henry always looked at you? That was the real deal."

"Plus," Maddy added, "even though I'm not fully in Camp Henry yet, I've gotta admit ... when it was good, it sounded really good." She shrugged. "And good isn't easy to come by."

"Good isn't enough," I said, though my voice wavered. "Not after everything that happened."

"Sure," Ivy agreed. "But maybe good could be the start of something better—if you're not too stubborn to give it a chance."

I thought about how he'd held me last night like I was something precious he'd found again. "Maybe."

"Only one way to find out," Maddy sing-songed.

"By not running away before he wakes up?" I sighed.

"Exactly!"

I glanced at my phone. "I should probably head back."

"To face the music?" Ivy grinned.

"To face my mother, who saw his car outside all night."

They winced in sympathy.

"Could be worse," Maddy offered. "Remember when my mom caught me and Jake Morrison making out in the wine cellar?"

"Wasn't that how you learned Gloria keeps a Super Soaker behind the bar?" Ivy asked.

"Why do you think I'm still single? Trauma like that leaves scars."

Laughing, I stood to leave. "Thanks, guys—for everything."

"That's what we're here for." Ivy hugged me tight. "Now go get your man."

"And maybe grab a romance novel on your way up," Maddy called after me. "For inspiration!"

The bell chimed behind me as I stepped into the morning sunshine. River Bend was energetic, the streets humming with the usual morning crowd. I squared my shoulders and returned to the bookstore, doing my best to ignore the glint of amusement in Mrs. Patterson's eyes as I passed.

Mom was helping a customer when I slipped in, but she still caught my eye with a look that said we'll talk later. I grabbed a romance novel from the new releases display— something about a second chance with a billionaire because apparently the universe has a sense of humor—and headed upstairs.

My apartment was quiet when I opened the door. Too

quiet. My heart sank as I realized Henry must have left. But there, on the kitchen counter, was a note.

I had to run to a meeting, but last night was perfect. Would you like to have dinner with me tonight? I promise to earn back all the trust you're willing to give me.

Henry

There seems to be a lack of your once-favorite romance novels. I always believed the real thing was better than fiction. But if you're willing to rewrite our story, I promise to make it a bestseller.

I pressed the note to my chest, fighting a grin. Maybe Ivy was right. Maybe it was time to stop running and give happy endings a chance.

Starting with dinner.

CHAPTER NINETEEN

Henry

I was halfway to Mason's office when my phone rang. James's nurse's number flashed on the screen, and my stomach dropped. She never called this early.

"Mr. Kingston? You need to come to Madison Center right away. Your grandfather..." She hesitated. "There's been a change in his condition."

I made an illegal U-turn, my heart pounding. "What kind of change?"

"He's asking for you. And..." Another pause. "We've called your mother."

The rest of her words blurred as I pressed the accelerator. I'd planned to meet Mason to determine where his loyalties lay in this fight against my father. But none of that mattered now.

Something was off the moment I stepped into James's room. The morning sun poured through the windows as usual, but his chair by the window, always occupied at this hour, sat empty. Instead, he remained in bed—a sight entirely unlike him.

"Grandfather?" I approached quietly, noting how pale he looked against the white sheets.

His eyes blinked open, taking a moment to focus. "Henry." His voice was weaker than usual, but the familiar warmth was still there. "I was starting to think you'd forgotten about me."

"Never." I sat beside him, ignoring how my stomach knotted at his appearance. "How are you feeling?"

"Like I'm tired of people asking me how I'm feeling." He attempted to sit up, and I hurried to help adjust his pillows. "Tell me something interesting instead. How's Savvy?"

Heat crept up my neck. "She's... We're..."

"Ah." His eyes twinkled with familiar mischief. "That good, hmm?"

"Grandfather—"

"I may be dying, Henry, but I'm not dead yet." He patted my hand. "And I'm not blind either. I see the way you look at her. The way she looks at you when she thinks no one's watching."

A nurse appeared in the doorway, her professional demeanor slipping as her eyes flicked to the monitors. She frowned at the numbers, jotting quick notes in his chart with a practiced efficiency.

"I need to speak with Dr. Harrison," she said, her voice neutral. "Mr. Kingston, would you mind stepping into the hall for a moment?"

James's hand shot out, gripping my wrist with surprising strength. "Whatever needs to be said can be said here. I've never been one for secrets."

The nurse hesitated, then nodded. "Your latest readings are concerning. The blood pressure—"

She stopped as James went rigid, his face going slack.

"Grandfather?" Alarm shot through me as his eyes lost focus. "I need help in here!"

The next few minutes were chaos. More nurses rushed in, followed by doctors speaking in rapid medical short-hand. Words like "pressure" and "bleeding" filtered through my panic. Someone tried to usher me out, but James's grip on my wrist remained firm.

"Stay," he commanded, his voice suddenly clear. "There are things you need to know."

The doctor hesitated, then nodded. "Five minutes. Then we need to run tests."

When we were alone again, James's eyes locked onto mine with fierce intensity. "Listen, Henry. In my desk, there's a blue folder. Everything you'll need is there—my lawyer's contact information, the trust documents, the people you'll need to talk to. I've been preparing for this longer than your father knows."

"Grandfather, don't—" My voice cracked. "You can rest. We can talk about this later."

"No." He squeezed my wrist. "No more later. Richard thinks he's dealing with a sick old man, but I've made sure you'll have what you need." His breath hitched. "Promise me you'll do what's right by everyone."

"I promise." My eyes burned. "But you're going to help me, right? You'll—"

"Where is she?" He looked around suddenly, confusion clouding his features. "Savvy should be here."

"I'll call her," I said. "I'll get her right now."

But when I reached for my phone, his grip tightened. "Not yet. First, you need to know..."

His voice faded as his eyes slipped closed.

Mom arrived minutes later, still in her yoga clothes, her face pale with fear. "Daddy?" she whispered, rushing to his bedside.

The next hours passed in a blur of medical terms and waiting rooms. Brain bleed, they said. It's common with his condition. Moving too fast for surgical intervention. I could only sit there, watching the man who'd been my constant slip away.

My phone buzzed periodically—Savvy, probably wondering why I hadn't called after leaving this morning. But every time I reached for it, something else demanded attention. Another doctor with questions about James's history. A nurse needing insurance information.

James drifted in and out of consciousness. Mom held his hand, singing softly—the lullaby she said he used to sing to her as a child. During one clear moment, he gripped my hand and said, "Don't wait for her to trust you, Henry. Show her who you are."

"I will," I promised. "Stay with me a little longer."

My father arrived around sunset, his presence casting a familiar weight over the room. But James didn't acknowledge him. Instead, his eyes found mine one last time.

"The folder," my grandfather whispered. "Remember."

Those were his last words.

The machines started their frantic beeping as his hand went slack in mine. I barely registered the doctors rushing in, the nurse gently pulling us back. Mom's anguished cry pierced the chaos as she clung to her father's hand.

"Time of death, 8:47 p.m."

The words echoed in the sudden silence, made more final by the absence of beeping monitors. My mother's sobs filled the void, but I couldn't move. Couldn't breathe.

Couldn't process that James Morrison—the only person who'd ever truly understood me—was gone.

"I'll handle the arrangements," my father said, reaching for his phone.

"No." My voice sliced through Mom's quiet sobs. "You're not handling anything."

"Henry." His voice carried that unmistakable warning edge. "This isn't the time—"

"When is the time, Dad? After you've complained about the cost of his care again? Or are you too busy calculating how much power Mom's inheritance will add to your empire?"

A shadow passed over his face. "You have no idea what you're talking about. Everything I've done—"

"Has been about control. Always." The words poured out, years of watching him diminish James fueling my anger. "You put him in here because you couldn't control him at home. Because he saw through you."

"I put him here because it was best for everyone," he snapped. "The cost alone—"

"The cost?" I laughed. "That's all he ever was to you. A line item on your balance sheet. The price of keeping Mom's father somewhere you could manage him."

"How dare you question—"

"He was worth ten of you." My voice shook. "He understood what genuine power was. It's not about money, control, or forcing people to bend to your will. It's about what you protect. What you nurture. What you love."

"Love?" He sneered. "Love doesn't build empires, Henry."

"No. But it builds things that last." I looked at my mother, still clutching James's hand. "Things worth fighting for."

"And what exactly are you fighting for? That little town? That girl?" His lip curled. "I thought we dealt with that weakness years ago."

The casual cruelty in his voice crystallized everything. "We're done," I said. "Whatever power you think you're about to gain, whatever plans you're making—I want no part of it. Not anymore."

"Don't be dramatic. Once your mother inherits—"

"You still don't get it, do you?" I turned away. "Some things can't be bought or controlled. James taught me that. It's a shame you never learned."

I stumbled out of the room, down endless corridors that were too bright, too sterile. My phone showed seven missed calls from Savvy and three texts asking if everything was okay. The last one sent a knife through my chest:

SAVVY

Some things never change.

THE DRIVE to River Bend passed in a blur, my vision clouded by tears I couldn't stop. I'd cried the entire way— for James, for the years stolen from us by my father's "care," for all the moments we'd never have.

Main Street was quiet, and most shops were dark except for the warm glow from River Bend Books. My hands shook as I climbed the familiar stairs to her apartment, barely able to see through fresh tears. I probably looked like hell—red-rimmed eyes, tear-stained cheeks, completely undone. But none of that mattered. I needed her.

The door swung open with force, but the anger burning in her expression froze when she saw my face. Her eyes

165

were red and swollen, too—she'd clearly been crying, though for a different heartbreak. She thought I'd abandoned her again, while I'd been watching my world collapse.

CHAPTER TWENTY

Savvy

"He's gone." Henry's voice broke on the words. "James is..."

I didn't let him finish. I pulled him inside, and he came willingly, like a ship finding a harbor in a storm. His body shook with silent sobs as I wrapped my arms around him. All my anger from the past hours—the unanswered calls, the fear of being ghosted again—melted away at the sight of his pain.

He buried his face in my neck, his tears hot against my skin. My fingers threaded through his hair, holding him closer as grief wracked his body. We stood like that for what seemed like hours until his breathing steadied.

When he lifted his head, his eyes were dark with need. The kiss started gentle—seeking comfort—but quickly blazed into something more desperate. His hands tangled in my hair as he backed me against the wall, pressing into me like he needed to feel anything other than loss.

"Savvy," he breathed against my mouth. "I need..."

"I know," I whispered, pulling him closer. "I'm here."

Our clothes fell away in desperate layers, hands seeking skin, needing to feel connected.

When he lifted me, I hooked my legs around his waist, gasping as he pressed me firmly against the wall. His lips ignited a fire down my neck, across my collarbone, lingering on every sensitive spot he hadn't forgotten.

His mouth captured mine again, urgent and searching. The salt of his tears lingered on my lips, and his hands explored my body, a silent plea wrapped in desperation. Each touch held him together, pulling him back from the edge of his grief.

"You're so warm," he murmured, his lips brushing my skin. "So alive." His voice broke, raw and unsteady, and I tugged him closer, wrapping myself around him like I could shield him from the depth of his pain.

"I've got you," I whispered, running my fingers through his hair. "I'm right here."

He carried me to the bed, but instead of the urgent passion from before, his movements turned almost reverent. His hands and mouth mapped my body like he was memorizing every inch, every reaction. Like he needed proof that life continued, that love survived, that some things couldn't be taken away.

"Savvy," he breathed out my name like a prayer. "I need to feel you. Need to know this is real."

I drew him down to me, cradling his face in my hands. His eyes were still bright with tears, but there was something else there too—a desperate hope. When I kissed him, soft and sure, he melted into me with a broken sound that was half sob, half moan.

He pressed against me, steady and sure. I pulled him closer, my body responding instinctively as his hands moved over my skin, drawing invisible patterns that soothed and ignited all at once. Each touch was a reminder, a return to something I'd almost forgotten. When we came together, the sound he made was raw, a broken exhale that carried the depth of his need.

"Look at me," I whispered, and his eyes found mine. The vulnerability there took my breath away. All his walls were gone—no defenses, no masks—just Henry, raw and unguarded in every way that mattered.

You feel like hope," he murmured, his movements slow and deliberate. "Like something I didn't think I'd find again." His forehead pressed to mine as we moved together, sharing breath, sharing heartbeats.

I held him tighter as his control slipped, as grief and desire tangled into something primal and necessary. His rhythm grew more urgent, more desperate, but his eyes never left mine. In them, I saw everything—loss and love, pain and hope, endings and beginnings.

"I've got you," I promised again as he shuddered against me. "Let go, Henry. I'll catch you."

He buried his face in my neck as he shattered, my name tumbling from his lips, raw and aching. I followed right after, clinging to him as waves of pleasure blurred into the salt of fresh tears—his or mine. I couldn't tell any more.

Afterward, he stayed wrapped around me, his head on my chest like he needed to hear my heartbeat. My fingers moved through his hair as his breathing slowly steadied.

"I should have called," he whispered. "When it started happening, I should have—

"Shh." I pressed a kiss to his temple, my voice soft but steady. "Tell me about him. Tell me everything. Maybe it'll help—remembering the good parts."

He adjusted his position but kept his head over my heart, as though the steady rhythm was the only thing keeping him sane. "He kept asking for you near the end. Said he wanted to see you one last time"

His voice cracked, the words tumbling out in a rush. "It happened so fast. I wanted to call you, but there wasn't time. One minute he was there, and the next..." He buried his face against my chest, his breath hitching as the memory consumed him.

His words left me momentarily speechless, but I forced myself to ask, "What happened?"

"Brain bleed," he said hoarsely. "The doctors said it was common with his condition, but God, Savvy. I wasn't ready. One minute he was lucid, telling me about a folder, and the next..." His arms tightened around me like he was holding on for dear life.

I stroked his hair, feeling the wet warmth of his tears against my skin. "Tell me something good. A memory."

His voice carried a touch of nostalgia. "He used to play chess with me every Sunday, even after he moved to Madison Center. He'd let me win sometimes, but only if I earned it. Said character wasn't built on easy victories."

"That sounds like James," I murmured, my voice breaking.

"He never forgot about you," he continued softly. "Had a first edition of *Jane Eyre* on his bedside table. Said it reminded him of you—a strong woman who wouldn't let the world break her spirit."

Fresh tears spilled down my cheeks. "He was the only one in your family who ever saw me."

"No." Henry pushed up on his elbow, his eyes finding mine in the dim light. "I saw you, but I wasn't brave enough to fight for what I saw."

"Henry—"

"He made me promise to do the right thing. I think he

meant by you and this town and everything that means something." His fingers traced my cheek. "I won't fail him this time. I won't fail you."

I drew him back down to me, needing his warmth as memories and grief tangled together. "Did he suffer?"

"No." Henry's voice was rough against my shoulder. "He was making plans right until the end."

"That's who he was." My fingers traced patterns on his back, feeling the strain in his muscles. "A quiet guardian."

"My father showed up at the end." His body went rigid. "Started talking about arrangements, about Mom's inheritance, like James was just another asset to acquire."

"What did you do?"

"I told him we were done. That James understood what actual power was—not control or money, but love. The things worth protecting." He lifted his head, his eyes finding mine in the darkness. "I walked away from all of it. The inheritance, the empire, everything he thinks matters."

"Are you okay with that?"

"For the first time in my life, I am." His hand cupped my cheek. "James left me something better than money. He left me the truth about who I could be."

The vulnerability in his voice made my heart ache. I pulled him closer, wrapping myself around him like I could shield him from the world's sharp edges.

"When I saw your text," he whispered, "you must have thought I was disappearing again... God, Savvy, I'm so sorry."

"You came back," I said. "That's what matters."

"I'll always come back to you." He pressed his lips to my temple. "You're my home."

"Tell me what you need," I whispered, running my fingers through his hair. "Anything."

"Just this." His arm tightened around my waist. "Just you. Holding me, letting me hold you. Making me feel like the world isn't ending."

A car passed outside, headlights briefly painting shadows across my ceiling. In the quiet that followed, I could hear the distant sound of the Hudson, eternal and unchanging.

"I keep thinking about all the things I should have said to him," Henry murmured. "I love him."

"He knew." I pressed a kiss to his forehead. "Trust me, Henry. He knew."

"Did you know he used to slip books under my door when my father grounded me?" Amusement colored his voice. "Adventure stories, mostly. Said every prison needs an escape route."

My heart clenched. "That sounds like James."

"He did the same for my mother when she was young. It was their secret language—the books they shared. Each one carried a message." His fingers traced idle patterns on my skin. "I think that's why he loved you so much. You understood that language."

Fresh tears slipped down my cheeks. "I loved him too."

"I know." He propped himself up to look at me. In the dim light, his eyes were dark pools of emotion. "Can I ... would it be okay if I stayed tonight? I don't think I can face going home yet."

"Of course." I pulled him back down, tangling our bodies together. "Sleep. I've got you."

He settled against me, his breath warm on my neck. For a while, we lay there, listening to the quiet sounds of the night—the distant train whistles, the rustle of autumn leaves, the steady rhythm of our hearts finding peace together.

"Your mom will worry," I murmured, though I made no move to let him go.

"I texted her before I came here." His voice was rough with exhaustion. "She understands. I think ... I think she always understood about us. Even when my father couldn't."

I ran my fingers along his spine, feeling the tightness slowly ease from his muscles. "What happens now?"

"Tomorrow, I'll stop by James's to grab that folder he mentioned, go through his things if needed." His arm tightened around me. "But tonight, I just want to remember how to breathe."

The vulnerability in his voice coursed through me. I pressed closer, trying to wrap him in all the comfort I could offer. His heartbeat steadied against mine, our breathing synchronizing in the darkness.

"You know what's strange?" he whispered after a while. "I keep thinking about that chess set in his study. The one he taught me on. How the pieces are probably still set up from our last game." His voice caught. "We never finished it."

"Oh, Henry." I kissed his temple, tasting salt.

"I don't want to finish it," he admitted. "As long as the game isn't over, some part of him is still..."

When his voice trailed off, I held him tighter, feeling fresh tears dampen my skin. We lay like that until his breathing evened out, sleep claiming him. But I stayed awake, keeping watch over his dreams, protecting him the only way I could.

In the distance, a train whistle echoed—long and mournful, like a farewell. Or maybe a beginning. Sometimes it was hard to tell the difference.

CHAPTER TWENTY-ONE

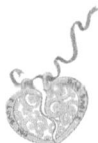

Henry

I woke to unfamiliar shadows on the ceiling, and Savvy's warmth curved against me. For a moment, I breathed her in, letting everything settle—James's death, the revelations, finding my way back here. Her alarm clock read 6:42, red numbers cutting through the grey dawn light filtering through her curtains.

"Hey," she murmured, turning in my arms. Her eyes were soft with sleep, but I caught their concern. The same look she'd given me last night when I showed up at her door, broken open by grief.

"I need to go to Madison Center," I said. "I can't ... I don't think I can face it alone. Would you come with me?"

She traced my jaw with gentle fingers. "Of course."

"I'll have to stop by my place first though. I need to change clothes." I couldn't quite meet her eyes, afraid she might see how much I needed her there.

"Let me make us coffee for the drive," she said, pressing a kiss to my shoulder before slipping out of bed. She pulled on my discarded shirt, and something in my heart ached at the sight—not desire, but a bone-deep longing for all the mornings we'd lost.

"We should probably add eating something to the plan," she said, and I realized I couldn't even remember my last meal. Everything before last night seemed distant, shrouded in a haze.

The familiar rhythm of her morning routine drifted through the walls—coffee maker gurgling, shower running. I found my pants and checked my phone. Three missed calls from Father. I turned it off.

After she finished, I wandered into her bathroom, the small space still steamy and warm. Her wild array of products covered every surface, somehow chaotic and homey. A fresh toothbrush sat on the counter, still in its package. The simple thoughtfulness of it made my throat tight.

Two cups of coffee later, we were navigating morning traffic, her hand resting on my knee. Her steady presence beside me kept the darker thoughts at bay. As I pulled up to my building, preparing to enter the underground garage, she looked up at the gleaming tower with an expression I couldn't quite read.

"What?" I asked, killing the engine.

"It's..." She paused, choosing her words. "This isn't you, Henry. This whole place—it's like a stage set where some version of you has been performing. But it's not real. Not really."

The elevator ride was silent, each floor taking us higher into a life I'd been pretending to want. When I opened my apartment door, its sterile perfection hit me through her eyes—the untouched leather furniture, the abstract art chosen by a decorator, and the kitchen that had never cooked an actual meal.

"I hate it," I said suddenly, the words escaping before I could stop them. "I hate every inch of this place."

"Then why stay?"

"Because it was easier than admitting I made a mistake." I moved to the window, looking out at the city sprawled below. "Easier than facing what I walked away from."

She joined me, her reflection a ghost in the glass. "And now?"

"Now?" I turned to face her. "Now I'm done with easy. Done pretending." I caught her hand and intertwined our fingers. "I'll call the realtor today. List it."

"Henry—"

"You were right. This place, everything in it—it's a shell I've been hiding in. The best parts of me only exist when I'm with you."

She squeezed my hand, and for a moment we stood there, surrounded by the evidence of my false life, finding something real in each other.

"I know a place," she said. "For breakfast. Around the corner."

"Murphy's?" I asked. "With those greasy eggs you love?"

"The same." Her eyes met mine in a challenge. "Unless you're still too good for diner coffee."

"I'm not good for much of anything right now." The admission came out raw but necessary. "But I'd love some terrible eggs with you."

Murphy's hadn't changed—same cracked vinyl booths, same coffee strong enough to strip paint. We slid into an old booth by the window, and for a moment, it was as if no time had passed.

"Still drowning your eggs in hot sauce?" I asked as she doctored her plate.

"Still pretending dry toast is a proper breakfast?" she countered.

The familiarity of it all—her stealing sips of my coffee, the way she knew exactly how many sugar packets I wanted —brought back a piece of myself I thought I'd lost.

After breakfast, we headed toward Madison Center. Each mile weighed heavier, reality pressing down again. But Savvy's hand found mine across the console, keeping me here, keeping me with her.

"I should check in at the desk," I said as we entered the care center. The morning shift nurse—Sarah, who'd been kind to James—looked up with sympathy.

"Mr. Kingston. I heard. I'm so sorry for your loss."

I swallowed hard, grateful for Savvy's hand slipping into mine. "We need to..." I couldn't finish the sentence.

"Of course." Sarah nodded in understanding. "Take all the time you need."

The elevator ride and the walk down the hallway stretched on endlessly. When we reached 517, I hesitated at the door.

"Together?" Savvy whispered.

I nodded, and we stepped inside.

His scent hit me first—Earl Grey and old books. But something was off. The room seemed emptier somehow, though nothing had been moved yet.

Savvy's hand tightened around mine as we walked farther in. The morning sun poured through the windows, casting long shadows across his empty chair.

"We can pack everything if you'd like," Sarah said gently from the doorway.

I nodded, unable to form words. Everything around me seemed too vivid, too painfully real.

Savvy moved toward the shelves, her fingers trailing

over the spines. "He used to tell me stories about these," she said softly. "Each first edition had its own history and reason for being here."

"He loved that you understood that." I joined her, remembering countless afternoons spent in this room. "He said you saw the magic in old books, not their value."

I moved to his desk, remembering his urgent words from yesterday. The blue folder was exactly where he said it would be. Inside, as he promised, were his lawyer's contact information, trust documents, and a list of names—people he'd trusted to help protect his legacy.

For a moment, we stood there, breathing in his essence —the lingering scent of Earl Grey, the familiar musty sweetness of his beloved books, that trace of mint from the candies he kept by his chair. Each detail a knife to my heart.

But we couldn't stay long. Not with Father making calls and setting things in motion. He wouldn't even wait for James to be buried before he started dismantling everything my grandfather had built.

"We need to go," I said, my voice rough. "There's not a minute to spare."

Savvy squeezed my hand, understanding in her eyes. "Your father's already making his move, isn't he?"

"Yes." I clutched the folder tighter. "I'm sure."

Back at Savvy's apartment, we spread the documents across her kitchen table.

My phone buzzed—Father, again. I sent it to voicemail just as Savvy's phone lit up. She stared at the screen, and I watched her face change, something shuttering behind her eyes.

"Dr. Blake," she said. The professional mask I remembered from yesterday slipped into place. "She's offering me another chance. Says my track record before this week was impeccable."

I saw her fingers tighten on the phone. "What are you thinking?"

"That I have student loans due next week." She laughed, but it held no humor. "That being Jennifer Walsh paid much better than being Savvy Honeysucker ever did."

Her eyes drifted to the stack of loan statements on her desk—the real reason she'd built her career around other people's endings. The money had been good. Great, even. Enough to keep the collectors at bay, enough to maintain her independence.

"But after everything..." She gestured between us at the scattered evidence of my father's schemes, at the ghost of James that seemed to linger in every memory. "How can I go back to that? To being that cold, perfect professional who makes endings easy?"

I reached for her hand across the papers, remembering all the times I'd wished I could explain why I left, all the clean breaks that had left us both raw. "Then don't."

"It's not that simple. These payments don't go away because I want a different life."

"No," I agreed. "But maybe it's time we both stopped running from what matters—time we faced the hard things together."

She stared at her phone, at Dr. Blake's message offering a way back to financial security. Back to Jennifer Walsh, the untouchable professional who never let anything touch her heart.

"I built this business around helping people avoid pain," she said, her voice quieter now. "Around making it easy to walk away."

I nodded, meeting her gaze. "But has it worked? Has it made things easier for you?"

She hesitated, her lips pressing into a thin line before she spoke again. "Maybe some things aren't supposed to be easy. Maybe the hard conversations are the ones worth having."

I reached for her, pulling her gently into my arms. A shudder ran through her, and I held her tighter, trying to steady her. Her voice broke the silence between us. "I'm scared."

"Of what?" I asked softly.

"Of making the wrong choice again," she whispered, pulling back just enough to meet my eyes. "Of building another life that isn't real." Her breath caught as she went on. "When you left, I created Jennifer Walsh because being Savvy Honeysucker hurt too much. And it worked. The money was good, the job kept me busy, and if there was an emptiness sometimes ... at least I was holding the reins."

"And now?"

"Now?" She glanced at her phone on the table. "Now I don't know who I am anymore. Jennifer Walsh would never have lost control of delivering a client's goodbye. She won't be standing here wondering if there's more to life than perfect exits."

"Maybe that's not a bad thing," I said. "Maybe it's time Savvy Honeysucker came back."

"I'm not that girl anymore, Henry." Her voice cracked. "I can't be that bright-eyed dreamer who thought love conquered all."

"No," I agreed, brushing a strand of hair from her face. "You're stronger now. Wiser. You've built something impressive, even if it started from pain."

"Built on quicksand," she muttered. "One crack in my

perfect facade, and Dr. Blake was ready to drop me. And without her referrals..."

"Then we'll figure something else out."

Her laugh held a sharp edge. "We? Last I checked, these student loans have my name on them, not yours."

"Savvy—"

"No." She stepped back, crossing her arms. "I can't let you solve this, Henry. I won't trade dependence on Dr. Blake for dependence on you. I need to figure this out myself."

I waited, watching her pace the small space between the kitchen and living room. This was the Savvy I remembered—fierce and independent, never wanting to be saved.

"What if," I said, "it wasn't about dependence? What if it was about choosing what you want, not what you need?"

She stopped pacing, her brow furrowed. "What do you mean?"

"I mean, forget the loans for a minute. Forget Dr. Blake. What would you choose if you could do anything and be anyone?"

She stood still, her gaze distant. Then, almost too softly, she said, "I'd help people walk into love, not walk away from it. I'd..." She let out a sudden laugh, shaking her head. "God, I sound like a Hallmark movie."

"You sound like yourself," I said, my voice steady. "The real you, not Jennifer Walsh."

Her phone buzzed again—another message from Dr. Blake. This time, Savvy didn't even glance at it.

"I can't quit," she said. "Not completely. Not yet. But maybe ... maybe I could be more selective. Take only the cases where walking away is the right answer, not just the easy one."

"And the loans?"

"Will still be there." She squared her shoulders, her voice growing steadier. "But maybe being Jennifer Walsh isn't the only way to pay them."

I wanted to argue, to offer help, to fix everything. But I knew that wasn't what she needed. Not from me, not anymore.

"Whatever you decide," I said instead, "I'm here. Not to save you or solve things. Just … here."

She nodded, then picked up her phone. I watched as she typed a response to Dr. Blake, her fingers moving purposefully. When she set it down again, something had changed in her expression—like she'd put down a weight she'd carried too long.

"I told her I need time," she said. "That I'm reevaluating my practice."

"And?"

"And maybe it's time to help people believe in something again." She looked up at me, her eyes clear and determined. "Some endings aren't meant to be easy, but beginnings—they're worth fighting for."

CHAPTER TWENTY-TWO

Savvy

I watched Henry's hands curl into fists at his sides, but his face remained tranquil.

His mother touched his arm—a silent reminder to keep his composure. Victoria Kingston was the picture of dignified mourning in her black dress and pearls, but there was steel beneath her grace. I'd seen that same quiet determination in James.

The service itself passed in a blur of hymns and remembrances. I sat in the back, letting the words wash over me as sunlight filtered through the stained glass, painting rainbow patterns across the wooden pews. Someone read from Ecclesiastes—a time for everything under heaven. A time to be born, a time to die. A time to break down and a time to build up.

My throat tightened as Henry stepped to the pulpit. He looked impossibly young in his dark suit, the loss visibly etched in his posture. His voice, when it came, was steady but raw with emotion.

"My grandfather understood the power of stories," he began. "He believed they could bridge any gap, heal any wound if we were brave enough to tell them honestly." His eyes found mine briefly in the crowd. "He taught me that strength isn't in what we own or control, but in what we protect. What we cherish."

Richard moved in his seat, his perfect mask of grief slipping for a moment. I recognized that look—the calculation behind the compassion. I'd seen it in countless clients who viewed relationships as transactions.

After the service, the crowd slowly dispersed into the crisp autumn afternoon. I lingered near the church steps, watching Henry accept more condolences with growing weariness. When Richard approached him, I moved closer, some protective instinct drawing me forward.

"Son," Richard began, his voice pitched for maximum sympathy. "Your grandfather and I may have had our differences, but I want you to know—"

"Save it." Henry's voice was quiet but sharp enough to cut glass. "We both know exactly who you are and what you want. But this isn't the time or place."

Richard looked at me, his eyes narrowing. "Why is she here? This is a family matter."

"Miss Honeysucker is included in the will," Victoria said smoothly, satisfaction in her voice. "James was quite specific about her presence being required."

The muscle in Richard's jaw ticked—a tell I'd seen in countless clients when their perfect plans started unraveling. "Included in the..." His face flushed with barely contained rage. "She hardly knew him."

"Quality over quantity, Richard dear," Victoria said, her voice honey-sweet, but her eyes hard as diamonds. "The lawyer is waiting. We shouldn't keep him."

The will was read in Todd Whitman's downtown office —a place that smelled of leather and old paper, its walls lined with leather-bound law books. I sat near the back again, watching Richard's shoulders tense. His mask of grief had slipped, revealing glimpses of the calculation beneath.

Mr. Whitman cleared his throat, adjusting his wire-rimmed glasses. "Before we begin, I want to note that James Morrison was exceedingly clear about his wishes. Everything has been properly documented and witnessed."

Richard leaned forward with that predatory gleam returning to his eyes. My stomach clenched, remembering similar expressions on clients who thought they were about to win something.

The initial bequests were straightforward—personal items to friends and family and charitable donations to local causes. Then, Mr. Whitman paused, shuffling his papers with deliberate care.

"Regarding the Morrison family library, specifically the first edition collection." He glanced at me over his glasses. "James was most explicit about this. The entire collection is to be transferred to Miss Savannah Honeysucker."

The air left my lungs in a rush. Around me, the room erupted in murmurs. Richard's head snapped up, his mask cracking further.

"The books," Mr. Whitman continued, "are being delivered to your residence as we speak, Miss Honeysucker. James left specific instructions about their care."

My vision blurred with tears. James's precious books— his treasures, his legacy. He'd chosen me to protect them.

"Now, regarding the matter of family assets." Mr. Whitman's voice cut through the whispers. "As established in the Kingston-Morrison Agreement of 1995, and I quote: 'No party shall lay claim to familial wealth established prior to marriage, including but not limited to business holdings, property, and inherited assets.'"

The color drained from Richard's face as the implications sank in. James and Victoria had outmaneuvered him decades ago, protecting both families with a single document.

"Furthermore," Mr. Whitman continued, adjusting his glasses, "the Morrison holdings will be distributed as follows. Fifty-one percent to Henry Kingston, and forty-nine percent to Victoria Morrison Kingston, making Henry the primary shareholder of all Morrison business interests."

Richard's knuckles went white on his armrest, his facade collapsing.

"That's impossible," he snarled. "The Morrison fortune—"

"Remains exactly where it belongs," Victoria cut in, her voice calm and composed. "With the family. Just as the Kingston assets remain with theirs."

Henry caught my eye across the room, his expression shifting with something unreadable. James's chess game started long before we realized we were pieces on the board.

The rest of the reading passed in a blur of legal terms and asset distributions. When it was over, I slipped out, needing air and space to process everything that had happened.

When I made it home, the late afternoon sun had turned the streets golden. True to Mr. Whitman's word, dozens of packed boxes lined my apartment walls. Each one was labeled in James's precise handwriting: "Dickens First Editions," "Austen Collection," "Brontë Sisters."

My hands shook as I opened the nearest box. The familiar scent of old paper and leather rose, bringing a fresh wave of grief. These weren't just valuable books—they were pieces of James's heart, collected and preserved over decades.

Inside a first edition of *Jane Eyre,* I found an envelope with my name written in James's elegant script. The paper was heavy and expensive, and my vision blurred as I unfolded it.

My dear Savvy,

If you're reading this, then my last move has been played. These books have been my companions through many chapters of my life, but they deserve a new guardian now—someone who understands that stories are more than words on paper. They're bridges between hearts, between generations.

You entered our lives like a hero from one of those timeless stories, breaking down the walls we so meticulously built with your unwavering honesty and boundless heart. I know you've guided others to their endings, but your real gift lies in helping people discover their beginnings. These books are more than a collection—they're possibilities. Use them well. Build something wonderful.

With great affection,
James

A knock at my door startled me from my tears. When I opened it, Victoria Kingston stood there, elegant as ever in her mourning clothes.

She studied me for a long moment. "I hear you're quite skilled at ending things, Miss Honeysucker."

"I was," I said, caught off guard by her directness. "But I think I'm done with endings. I'm ready to help people find their beginnings instead."

Her lips curved—not warm, but expectant. "What about one last ending? For old times' sake?" She gestured toward the boxes lining my walls. "We need to talk about Richard, the future, and what James really left you."

I stepped back, letting her enter. Something in her expression told me this conversation would change everything.

Victoria moved through my small apartment with surprising grace, taking in the boxes of books lining every wall. Her fingers trailed over one labeled "Victorian Treasures" with something like affection.

"I'll be direct, Miss Honeysucker. I want to hire you for one last job." She turned to face me, her eyes sharp with purpose. "I'm leaving Richard. After James's death, I realize I can't let him destroy anything else I love."

My gaze drifted to the *Jane Eyre* first edition, James's letter still tucked inside. Help people find their beginnings, he'd written. Maybe this was mine.

"Richard will fight back," I said. "He won't go quietly."

Victoria's expression sharpened a glint of determination in her eyes. "Count on it. That's exactly what we need. Let him show everyone exactly who he is. In public. Where he can't hide."

She reached into her bag and pulled out a thick manila envelope, placing it on my coffee table. "Your student loans.

James kept meticulous records of everything Richard might try to use as leverage." She tapped the envelope. "Consider this hazard pay for one last job."

"I can't—it's too much," I protested, staring at the envelope.

"It's the cost of freedom—mine." Victoria's voice softened. "Some things are worth any price, Savvy. I learned that from James. Now I'm learning how to fight for it."

I picked up the envelope. "If I do this ... it's my last breakup job. Ever."

"Good," she said. "It's time for you to write different stories."

"When?" I asked.

"You pick the time and place," Victoria said, standing smoothly. "I'll tell him it's a meeting about merging assets. Make him think he still has a chance to get everything he wants."

A glimmer of satisfaction crossed my face. "I know exactly where to do this. And I know who can make sure the right people are there to witness his true colors." I could already picture it—the perfect stage for his final act. "Word travels fast in this town. If we set the scene right, the people who need to see Richard for who he really is will be there."

"Henry has everything you'll need," Victoria said, moving toward the door. She paused, her hand on the knob. "Savvy? Thank you. For understanding what needs to be done."

After she left, I stood among James's books—his legacy, his protection, his last gift. Outside, leaves skittered across my window, red and gold in the fading light. Somewhere in the distance, a train whistle echoed—wistful or hopeful. I couldn't tell anymore.

I picked up *Jane Eyre* again, running my fingers over its

worn leather spine. "Well, James," I whispered to the quiet room. "I guess we have one last story to tell. And this time, it's happening at Rise and Grind."

The books around me seemed to hold their breath, waiting for the next chapter to begin.

CHAPTER TWENTY-THREE

Henry

I came back here to feel close to him, to remember the man who had shaped everything I wanted to be. The hallway to Room 5 1 7 looked exactly the same—same bland artwork, same antiseptic smell, same squeak in the tile near the door. But when I pushed it open, the room beyond felt like stepping into a void.

Gone were the rich leather chairs, the towering bookcases, and all the warmth James had brought to this sterile place. The afternoon sun streamed through bare windows where his favorite curtains had once filtered the light. It had been reset to its original state—another place for someone else to wait out their final chapter.

An empty hospital bed dominated the room where his reading chair had been. The walls, stripped of their temporary personality, glowed an institutional white. It was amazing how quickly a life could be erased, packed away in boxes, leaving nothing but blank spaces behind.

"Mr. Kingston?" Sarah, the morning nurse, appeared in

the doorway. Her voice was gentle and understanding. "Sometimes it helps to remember them somewhere else, somewhere they really lived."

"No need," I said. "James isn't here anymore. He's in every building we'll save, every small business we'll protect." I touched the doorframe one last time. "He's in everything we're about to do."

I SPREAD the blueprints across the counter at *Rise and Grind* just as the lights flipped on and the first pot of coffee started brewing. The coffee shop had just opened, but Savvy knew the barista, and we'd come early to commandeer every table in the place before the morning rush.

By the time the board meeting started, there wouldn't be a single seat left unclaimed.

"The James Morrison Preservation Center," I said, tapping the architectural renderings. "A permanent foundation to protect River Bend's history while securing its future."

Mason whistled low, studying the plans. "Starting with Main Street?"

"Starting with hope." I pulled out the grant proposals. "Every historic building owner will have access to funds for modernization that preserves character. James said River Bend's heart was in its bones. Those bones are the people, and we aren't letting my father take this town."

"And the board meeting later?"

I fought to keep the grin off my face. "Make sure every table is filled. Not just with board members, but with everyone who makes River Bend what it is. Patterson's already working her magic on the guest list. By the time Richard walks in, he'll be outnumbered in his own game."

Mason smirked, shaking his head. "You're good."

"I learned from the best." I moved the blueprints, revealing the document beneath—the one establishing the foundation with my fifty-one percent share. "By this time tomorrow, River Bend's future will be secure. And Richard will show everyone exactly who he is."

I ran my finger along the edge of the foundation agreement, its weight pressing on me. This wasn't just about River Bend—it never had been. James always said that small towns like this were the heartbeat of something bigger, something worth protecting.

The foundation wasn't just a safeguard for River Bend but a shield for every historic small town fighting to survive in the shadow of corporate greed. It was about preserving the diners where people swapped stories over coffee, the mom-and-pop shops that knew your name, and the sidewalks where kids grew up playing tag. James believed those places weren't just relics of the past—they were the soul of the future.

And Richard? He'd do what men like him always did—grab for power, step on the people who couldn't fight back, and expose his true nature in the process.

I just had to make sure *everyone* was watching when it happened.

CHAPTER TWENTY-FOUR

Savvy

"What do you think, Commitment? Trust fund baby or corporate titan?" I stood before my breakup wardrobe, considering what Richard truly was. "This is job number three hundred and forty-six. The last one."

Commitment bubbled thoughtfully, his iridescent fins catching the morning light. Behind him, stacks of James's first editions lined my bedroom walls like silent witnesses.

"You're right." I reached past the dependable blue blazer I usually wore, pulling out the black power suit with its razor-sharp tailoring. "He's definitely a trust fund baby who thinks family money makes him untouchable. Time to teach him a lesson."

My phone buzzed—a text from Henry.

HENRY

Everything's ready. Mason's got the
seating arranged exactly how we planned.

I checked my reflection, adjusting the suit jacket's sleek

lapels. Sharp, uncompromising, and absolutely lethal. Perfect for taking down someone who thought money could buy anything—or anyone.

"You know what's funny, Commitment?" I dabbed on my signature red lipstick—armor, not allure. "All those perfectly orchestrated breakups, all those clean endings I crafted ... none of them were really clean. They were ... postponed messes."

The first edition of *Jane Eyre* caught my eye, James's letter still marking the page. I picked it up, the familiar feel of it grounding me. "But this one? This mess needs to happen. Right in the open where everyone can see the truth."

I pictured Rise and Grind in about two hours, packed with River Bend's finest—all the people Richard had tried to manipulate, now gathered for what would be his final act. The best part? He wouldn't even realize he was walking onto a stage.

Victoria had played him perfectly, feeding his ego just the right bait—a private meeting about merging assets, about finally getting his hands on what he'd always wanted: the Morrison money.

"What do you think he'll do when he sees me there instead of Victoria?" I asked Commitment, who flared his fins importantly. "Yeah, me too. He'll be shocked. Too focused on the threat right in front of him to see the trap closing."

I slipped James's letter into my blazer pocket, right over my heart. A reminder of why I was really doing this—not for money or revenge, but for legacy.

I checked the time—6:45. enough time to catch my usual train.

"Well, Commitment." I straightened my shoulders,

checking my reflection one more time. "Let's go write an ending worth remembering."

Joe was in his usual spot when I boarded, reaching for the tissue box he kept ready. I waved it away as I slid into my regular seat.

"I won't need those today," I said, smoothing my power suit. "This ending's going to be different."

He studied me for a moment, then his expression changing, amusement lighting his face. "About time," was all he said before moving down the aisle, calling out his familiar "Tickets, please!"

The familiar rhythm of the train helped steady my nerves as the countryside slipped past. I'd made this journey hundreds of times but today felt different. Today wasn't about cushioning someone else's fall. It was about justice. The same route I'd taken for countless breakups, but this time I wasn't Jennifer Walsh, professional heartbreaker. Today, I was just me—Savvy Honeysucker, ready to break up with the idea of breakups forever.

The walk from the station held a strange clarity. As I passed The Paper Crane, I glanced at the window—my emergency escape route from a different Kingston. Today, there would be no 911 texts to my friends. No hiding in a bathroom while my world unraveled.

Mason, who I'd met at the funeral, had the door open before I reached it. He didn't just stand in the entrance—he filled it, broad shoulders and sharp gaze making him look more like private security than legal counsel. The kind of man people instinctively stepped around.

"Everyone's in position," he said as I passed. "Board members in the window seats, town council by the counter, small business owners scattered throughout."

I nodded, taking in the careful choreography. Every

table filled with people whose lives Richard had tried to control, whose futures he'd tried to buy. All of them pretending to be absorbed in their coffee and phones. All of them waiting.

"His table?" I asked, though I already knew the answer.

"Center of the room." Mason tapped the table with deliberate precision. "Best sight lines for everyone."

I settled into what would be the power position: the chair facing the door.

A moment later, the bell above the door chimed exactly at nine. I watched Richard's expression shift from anticipation to confusion to barely controlled rage in the space of three seconds. His eyes locked onto me, not even registering the unusually full coffee shop.

"What are you doing here?" He tried to keep his voice low, professional, but the edge of panic bled through. "Where's Victoria?"

"Sit down, Richard." I gestured to the chair across from me, channeling every ounce of Jennifer Walsh's professional calm. "We need to talk."

"I have nothing to say to you." But he sat anyway, his body rigid with tension.

I removed an envelope from my folder and slid it across the table. "Here's a check for twenty-five thousand dollars. According to your prenup with Victoria, that's what you're entitled to. Your marriage is over."

When he didn't move to take it, I placed the second folder between us. "But we're not finished. River Bend is breaking up with you too. Every person you tried to bully, every business you attempted to pressure, every piece of property you schemed to acquire—they're all here to witness this ending."

"You can't..." Richard's fingers curled around the check,

crumpling it as he registered the unusual quiet in the coffee shop. His head jerked up, taking in the faces around him—people he'd threatened, manipulated, tried to buy. Board members who'd received his "generous offers." Shop owners he'd tried to pressure into selling. The town council members he'd attempted to bribe.

The blood drained from his face as realization dawned. Every person who had once feared him was here—and they didn't look afraid anymore.

"Actually, I can," I said, pulling out the board's letter. "Your company has completed its investigation into the allegations of wrongdoing tied to River Bend. Turns out, they found a striking pattern of abuse and manipulation. And now, they won't touch you with a ten-foot pole."

I let the weight of that settle before delivering the final blow.

"They'd like you to step down, Richard. Immediately. You're a liability they can't afford anymore. Consider this your official notice—your particular brand of hostile takeovers is no longer welcome."

"This is ridiculous!" Richard surged to his feet, sending his chair crashing backward. The crumpled check fell from his fingers to the table. "You can't possibly think—"

"That people would stand up to you?" I cut him off, my voice steady. "That your threats would stop working?" I gestured to our audience. "Look around, Richard. Really look. Everyone you attempted to manipulate, everyone you tried to bully or buy ... they're all here. And they're not afraid anymore."

Movement caught my eye. It was Marcus tensing behind the counter, ready to vault over it if needed. I gave him a slight wave without taking my eyes off Richard. I had this.

"She speaks the truth." Victoria's voice sliced through the heavy silence as she entered from the back room. "It's over, Richard. The marriage, the schemes, all of it."

The look on his face as reality sank in was something I'd remember forever—the moment a man who thought he held all the cards realized he'd been bluffing with an empty hand.

"This isn't over," he spat, but the threat sounded hollow.

"Actually, it is." My hand brushed James's letter in my pocket, drawing power from it. "You've taken enough, Richard. Years of mine and Henry's lives. The peace of mind of everyone in this room. You tried to steal the soul of a town for profit. But you won't take anything else."

Richard's face contorted with rage. Henry was suddenly there, his hand on Richard's shoulder.

"I think it's time for you to leave," he said.

The silence in Rise and Grind was absolute as Richard looked around, realizing his reign had ended.

When he spoke, his voice was barely controlled. "You'll regret this. All of you."

"No," I said simply. "We won't."

The bell chimed as he stormed out, the sound oddly cheerful in the heavy quiet. For a moment, no one moved. Then, like a dam breaking, the room erupted in conversation.

I sank back into my chair, my hands shaking as I gathered the documents. It was done. My last breakup, my last ending.

Henry appeared at my side, his hand warm on my shoulder. "Are you okay?"

I looked up at him, then at the crowd of people around us—all of them talking, laughing, some of them crying with relief. This was what a real ending looked like

—not clean and simple, but messy and real and full of possibility.

"Yeah," I said. "I think I am."

Through the window, I watched as Richard climbed into the back of his waiting town car, his driver pulling smoothly into the New York traffic. Somewhere in my apartment, Commitment was probably doing victory laps in his tank. I'd have to tell him all about it later, about how breakup three hundred and forty-six turned out to be less of an ending and more of a beginning for everyone.

CHAPTER TWENTY-FIVE

Henry—Three Months Later

"Just imagine it," Maddy said, spreading her hands against the dreary spring sky like she was framing a masterpiece. Her sleek black hair was pulled back in a precise ponytail, her slim dancer-like frame vibrating with barely contained excitement. "Fifty drones rising in perfect formation over the Hudson. The main group creates this gorgeous champagne bottle, while the secondary formation bursts outward in a celebration of lights."

"What could go wrong?" Mason muttered from his spot against the rental van.

Maddy looked at me before turning to Mason. "Why are you even here?"

Mason laughed. "I'm the best man, and given your history of proposal disasters, Henry thought it might be good to have a lawyer nearby."

"Those weren't disasters," Maddy interjected. "They were part of the learning curve. Besides, no one has lost a limb. A few feathers in the fountain, maybe a bride who took an unexpected swim, but nothing catastrophic."

"Yet," Mason said.

I chuckled, shaking my head. "In Maddy's defense, every great event planner has war stories. At least hers are memorable."

"This appears to be another in the making," Mason added. "There's an approaching storm, the wind off the river is fierce, and—" he eyed Maddy skeptically "—the fact that I heard about your last Valentine's Day event with the painted pigeons, I'm not convinced this will go smoothly."

Maddy spun to face him. "Those pigeons were a creative solution to a budget problem."

"Didn't they molt mid-flight? I heard you painted them pink and blue because white doves were too expensive, and the bride ended up looking like she'd been dive-bombed by a gender reveal party gone wrong."

"The colors represented the merging of two lives! His and hers."

The drone operators, a pair of increasingly nervous-looking guys, kept checking their tablets. The taller one spoke up. "Ms. Chen, about these wind conditions—"

Just then, Victoria pulled up with Savvy.

"The timing is perfect," Maddy insisted. "Get your bride and get her in place."

As I walked to meet Savvy, I heard Maddy's frantic whisper carrying across the deck: "No, no, that's not right—the wind is pushing them—"

Savvy kissed me and then stared at the drones. "What are you up to?"

I shrugged. "It's a surprise."

"Okay, something's wrong with that formation," Savvy said as we reached the overlook.

The drones, meant to create an elegant champagne bottle, drifted in the strengthening wind.

"That's, uh..." Mason's voice carried a mix of horror and amusement. "That's not a bottle anymore."

"Oh god." I watched as the wind pushed the formation into an unmistakably phallic shape hovering over the Hudson. "That's definitely not a bottle," I said.

Victoria cleared her throat delicately. "Well, I suppose this gives new meaning to a proposal going cockeyed."

"Henry Kingston," Savvy turned to me, laughter bubbling up, "did you try to propose to me with what appears to be a giant—"

"Penis," Maddy wailed from behind us. "It's a giant penis over the Hudson." She frantically waved at the operators. "Can't you adjust the—"

"If we move them now, in this wind—" The operator's warning was cut off by another gust that sent the drones spinning, making the formation even more anatomically correct.

"Someone posted this on River Bend's Facebook page," Mason announced, holding up his phone. "It's got twenty likes."

"The second formation!" Maddy screamed as the 'cork' section of drones activated. "Stop the second—"

It was too late. The programmed spray of celebratory lights burst from the top of the now decidedly phallic formation, creating an unmistakable display over the Hudson.

"Well," Savvy managed between fits of laughter, "that's certainly one way to make your proposal memorable."

"Did your drone display just..." Victoria paused delicately, "...climax over the river?"

"One hundred likes on Facebook," Mason updated, not

trying to hide his grin. "Someone commented, 'Most exciting proposal in River Bend history.'"

I dropped to one knee, figuring I might as well commit fully to this disaster. "Savvy Honeysucker, this is absolutely not how I planned to do this—"

"You mean you didn't plan to propose with an ejaculating drone penis over the Hudson?" Her eyes sparkled with mirth. "Because honestly, this is perfect."

I looked up at Savvy. The rain was falling, and a spectacular aerial malfunction was still going on above us, but I somehow found the perfect words.

"I had this whole elaborate plan. Romantic lights and a champagne bottle are exquisite. Instead, I've given River Bend its most memorable Facebook moment ever. But you know what? This feels right. Because loving you has been about finding the perfect in all our imperfect moments."

Behind us, I heard Maddy shriek as the final drone formation—meant to spell out 'Marry Me' in elegant lights—began spinning wildly. The lights flickered and jumped, creating a messy pattern.

"Oh, dear god," Mason muttered. "They're losing altitude."

The drones dropped one by one, some spinning toward the Hudson, others drifting in the strong wind. The message broke apart into a chaotic mess.

"I love you," I continued, ignoring the growing crowd of onlookers with their phones out. "Will you marry me?"

"Yes," Savvy said, laughing. "Yes, to the worst but best proposal ever."

As I slipped the ring on her finger, the drone formation lost its battle with the wind, scattering across the sky in what looked disturbingly like a grand finale.

"And THAT," Victoria announced dryly, "is what I call going out with a bang."

"Five hundred likes," Mason called out, shielding his phone from the rain. "And three local news stations want permission to run the footage."

The rain started pelting harder as I met her eyes, her face lit with excitement despite the storm soaking both of us. "Yes?" I asked, barely able to hear myself over the wind.

"Yes!" she shouted, laughing as she threw her arms around me. Her voice carried above the storm, her joy undeniable even as we were drenched.

"News vans," Maddy groaned, pointing toward the parking lot as we ran for cover. We dashed into Common Grounds, dripping water everywhere, just as reporters started spilling out of their vehicles with cameras raised.

"Five minutes," Maddy moaned, collapsing into a chair and letting her head thud onto the table. "Five minutes before this goes viral. My professional reputation..."

"Is about to explode?" Mason suggested, wringing out the hem of his shirt and earning a glare from Maddy that could have stopped the rain entirely.

"Actually," Savvy said, examining her ring while I wrapped my jacket around her shoulders, "this is marketing gold for your new business. Think about it—'No matter what goes wrong, we'll make it right.'" She paused. "Maybe leave out the part about the anatomically correct drone display."

The barista set down a round of celebratory hot chocolates. "On the house. That was the most entertaining thing I've seen in River Bend."

"A thousand likes," Mason announced, checking his phone. "And ... yep, someone tagged the Channel 4 news team."

"The Channel 4 team that Victoria's on the board with?" Savvy asked innocently.

Victoria lifted her perfectly made cappuccino, her eyes gleaming with amusement. "I may have texted them. This is exactly the kind of heartwarming local story they love." She paused, taking a sip. "Though we might want to describe it as a 'technical malfunction' rather than..."

"Rather than a drone dick?" Mason offered.

"Mason!" Maddy looked scandalized.

"What? I'm calling it what it is. Was. Before it..." he said, making an explosive hand gesture.

"So," I pulled Savvy closer, breathing in the scent of rain, coffee, and possibility. "When do you want to get married?"

Her eyes met mine, dancing with that mix of mischief and certainty that had made me fall in love with her. "How about tomorrow?"

"Your dad would kill me if he didn't get to walk you down the aisle."

"True." She laughed. "And what kind of wedding planner would I be if I eloped?" She twisted the ring on her finger. "How does summer sound? I think I can whip something together by then."

"You're already planning it, aren't you?"

"Of course, I am. And don't worry—" she nodded toward where Maddy was now trying to explain to a reporter that she was "revolutionizing proposal technology" while Mason made helpful hand gestures behind her back illustrating exactly what kind of revolution had occurred, "—we're definitely keeping the drones grounded this time."

"Two thousand likes," Mason said, scrolling through his phone. "And someone started a GoFundMe to 'Save the Love Drones.'"

"You know what this means," Savvy said, leaning into me as she watched another news van pull into the lot. "This is exactly the story I wanted for my business. Not only the perfect moments but the real ones. The ones that go hilariously wrong and end up better than any plan could have made them."

Victoria raised her cup in a toast. "To River Bend's most memorable proposal."

"Wait till the wedding," Maddy jumped in, looking up from her mortified slump. "I promise, no aerial displays of any kind."

"And no painted pigeons," Mason added.

"That was ONE TIME—"

I watched Savvy twist the ring on her finger—not the massive five-carat diamond my father kept in the family vault, but something that was purely her—rose gold, with a simple solitaire diamond held in delicate twisting vines. The moment I'd seen it, I'd known. Like I'd known with her.

The rain fell softly outside, a gentle contrast to the chaos of moments before. The river churned below, catching the last glimmers of light from the drowning drones, the water reflecting the messy, beautiful randomness of love. My mother's raised brow, Mason's quiet, shaking shoulders, and Maddy's wide-eyed mix of horror and pride blended into a moment that was impossibly, perfectly them.

Outside, the last drone gave up its fight with the storm, splashing into the Hudson like a final punctuation mark on history's most spectacular proposal failure.

It turned out that some love stories were born not in calm but in the beautiful wreckage of unexpected chaos.

CHAPTER TWENTY-SIX

Savvy – Three Months Later

"Stop fidgeting," Mom scolded, adjusting my veil for the hundredth time. "You'll wrinkle the silk."

I caught her hand, squeezing gently. "The silk survived thirty-two years in that preservation box. I think it can handle a few wrinkles."

Her wedding dress fit me perfectly, though we'd modernized it. The vintage lace still caught the June sunlight streaming through The Weathered Barn's restored windows, but now it hugged my curves in a way that would have scandalized 1991.

"Your father's pacing outside," Ivy announced, sweeping in with her makeup kit. For once, she wasn't the one wearing the outrageous bridesmaid dress—instead, she looked elegant in a deep blue silk that fit and didn't have a bustle. "I think he's having a crisis about his manicure."

I laughed, remembering the epic battle to get forty years of engine grease from under his fingernails. After three hours at Gloria's favorite spa, Dad had emerged looking distinctly traumatized but with hands that could touch white silk without leaving marks.

"How's the crowd?" I asked, trying to peek through the window without disturbing Mom's careful arrangement of my train.

"Full house," Maddy reported, joining us with a clipboard I was pretty sure was for show.

It struck me then—how easily we all moved around each other, how effortlessly we fit.

After months of wedding planning, last-minute disasters, and more than a few wine-fueled strategy sessions, we'd become something close to family. Even Mason, who'd initially treated all of this like one of his legal negotiations, had somehow ended up in the middle of everything—coordinating contracts, keeping the town gossip from derailing vendor agreements, and suffering through more group chats than any man should have to endure.

"Mrs. Patterson's crying, and we haven't even started. Also, she's live tweeting everything."

"Of course she is." I smoothed my hands over the vintage silk, remembering all the endings I'd orchestrated in designer suits with professional distance. Today was different—like stepping into my story instead of managing everyone else's.

"Mr. Dixon's in the front row," Ivy added, making minute adjustments to my mascara. "Looking surprisingly dapper for someone who usually dresses like he raided a thrift store in 1962."

"Did you know this place used to be River Bend's social center? Before it became, you know..."

"A glorified storage unit for his unsold antiques?" I finished, remembering all the times we'd passed by The

Weathered Barn, wondering what treasures lay buried under decades of dust.

"Speaking of which," Ivy's eyes sparkled with familiar mischief, "have you seen what he did with the entire space?"

I shook my head. We'd cleaned out enough room for the ceremony, but the back room had remained Mr. Dixon's domain.

"He cleared it all out," Maddy said excitedly. "Every single piece. He said it was his wedding gift to you—a blank canvas for whatever follows."

A knock at the door interrupted whatever she was about to say next. Dad poked his head in, and my breath caught. Paul Honeysucker, who I'd never seen in anything fancier than clean coveralls, stood in a perfectly tailored tux.

"Ready to do this, kiddo?" His voice was gruff with emotion, and I noticed the faint hesitation in his movements as he offered his elbow.

Dad squeezed my arm as we paused at the entrance. The Weathered Barn had been transformed—mason jars filled with fairy lights hung from rustic wooden beams, and wildflowers lined the aisle in copper pots that Dad had restored, each one polished to a mirror shine. White hydrangeas and blue delphiniums created a natural cascade, punctuated by sprays of Queen Anne's lace that reminded me of stars.

Henry stood waiting beneath an arch woven with ivy and white roses, and the moment our eyes met, everything else faded away. Even Mrs. Patterson's theatrical sobbing from the front row couldn't break the spell.

When Dad placed my hand in Henry's, he said, "Take care of my girl." His voice was rough with emotion, and I saw Henry blink back tears.

"Dearly beloved," Gloria began—we'd insisted she get ordained just for this—"we're gathered here today because these two got their act together."

Laughter rippled through the crowd as she continued, "And because sometimes the best love stories take the scenic route."

When it came time for our vows, Henry said, "Savvy Honeysucker, I spent five years trying to convince myself I could live without you. I was wrong. You are my north star, my harbor in every storm, my reason for fighting back when it would be easier to give in. I vow to spend every day making sure you never doubt that you're the best decision I've ever made." His voice carried clear and strong through the barn.

My hands rested in his as I began my own vows. "Henry Kingston, you crashed back into my life like a perfect storm, turning everything upside down in the best possible way. I promise to fight for us, to never take the simple path if it means walking away from you. I promise to love you through every imperfect, beautiful moment that lies ahead."

A warm June breeze carried the scent of roses through the barn's open doors as Gloria pronounced us husband and wife. When Henry kissed me, Maddy's "subtle" special effects—a cascade of silver streamers—went off early, showering everyone with sparkles. The timing was wrong but somehow perfect, like us.

After the streamers settled around us like silver rain, I squeezed Henry's hand. "Wait," I whispered. "I have something for you."

From a hidden pocket Ivy had expertly sewn into my dress, I pulled out a yellowed cocktail napkin, preserved despite the years. Henry's eyes widened in recognition as I unfolded a sketch of a little house by the river, complete with garden space and floor-to-ceiling bookshelves.

"You kept it." His fingers traced the faded lines. "All this time?"

"Maybe some part of me never stopped believing in that dream," I said softly. "Even when I was doing everything possible to prove I didn't need it."

Henry pressed his forehead to mine, the napkin caught between our clasped hands. "We can still build it, you know. All of it."

His laugh was thick with emotion as he carefully folded the memory into his jacket pocket, right over his heart.

Later, as we cut into the cake—a masterpiece of copper-painted tiers and handcrafted sugar flowers that matched my bouquet—Henry got frosting on my nose despite my best efforts to avoid it.

"The bouquet toss!" Ivy called out, gathering the single ladies. My wedding bouquet, a cascade of white roses and blue delphiniums tied with copper ribbon, sailed through the air in a perfect arc ... straight into Maddy's surprised hands.

"The garter's next!" someone shouted, and I caught Henry's wicked grin as he knelt before me. The delicate lace garter—borrowed from Mom and something blue—snapped across the room directly at Mason, who caught it reflexively.

"Don't even think about it," Maddy warned as Mason approached with the garter, though her cheeks flushed pink.

"Please," Mason drawled, though his ears had reddened. "I'd rather walk through Richard Kingston's hostile takeover again than be stuck in a room with your drone collection."

"Funny," Maddy shot back, clutching my bouquet like a

shield, "I was thinking I'd rather paint a thousand pigeons than attempt to dance with a lawyer who thinks a sense of humor is a liability."

But it was during the reception that the real magic happened. Mr. Dixon appeared at our table, looking uncomfortable in his Sunday best.

I watched Ivy try to convince Mrs. Patterson that she couldn't livestream the entire reception when Mr. Dixon approached our table. He pulled Henry aside, and I saw them exchange something—an envelope, maybe?—followed by matching grins that made me instantly suspicious.

After their hushed conversation, they both turned to me.

"Come with us," Henry said, extending his hand. "Mr. Dixon has something to show us."

Mr. Dixon led us through to a back room I barely recognized. The space had been completely cleared out, its soaring ceilings and original hardwood floors glowing in the evening light. "Took me three weeks to clear it all out," he said proudly, running a hand along one of the exposed beams. "But a deal's a deal, and I wanted it perfect for today."

Mr. Dixon's eyes grew wistful with memory. "Your grandmother used to plan all the town's celebrations here," he told me. "Back when River Bend knew how to throw a proper party. Been waiting for the right moment to pass it on to someone who'd bring that magic back."

"Pass it on?" I turned to Henry, who was holding out the envelope I had seen earlier.

"Happy wedding day, love," he said. "Mr. Dixon and I have been working on this for months."

My hands shook as I opened it. Inside was a deed—to

The Weathered Barn. My name was right there on the dotted line.

"You didn't," I breathed.

"I did." Henry's gaze warmed. "Every love story needs the right setting. And I thought maybe it was time for River Bend to have a place where happy endings are just the beginning."

"Oh my god!" Maddy's voice carried from the doorway where she and Ivy had been eavesdropping. "It's perfect! We could do everything here—proposals, weddings, celebrations—"

"A one-stop shop for happily ever afters," Ivy finished, moving through the space like she could see it all.

"Ever After, Inc.," I said, the name feeling right on my tongue. "Everything you need to make your perfect day perfect."

"Or perfectly imperfect," Henry added with a grin, no doubt remembering his own drone disaster of a proposal.

Mr. Dixon cleared his throat. "Well, I'll leave you young folks to it. Remember—this place has seen a lot of love stories. Treat her right."

As he walked away, Maddy was in full planning mode. "We'll need to update the wiring, maybe add some modern lighting, but keep the vintage charm."

"Slow down," I laughed. "I just got married. Maybe we can wait until tomorrow to start the next adventure?"

But looking around the space—at my best friends deep into plotting and planning, at Henry's look of quiet pride, and at the way the evening light bathed everything in shades of possibility—I knew this was exactly right. The Breakup Broker was officially retired, and something new was beginning.

A commotion from the main room drew our attention.

"Speaking of adventures," Ivy said with a grin, "I think Maddy's grand finale is about to start."

We hurried back in time to hear the first notes of "At Last" fill the air. But instead of the simple first dance we'd planned, the ceiling erupted in a shower of silver stars—actual metallic stars, drifting down on nearly invisible threads while tiny lights twinkled in the rafters.

"No drones," Maddy said when we stared at her. "You said no drones. But you didn't ban stars."

"Your stars are crooked," Mason called out as Maddy finished adjusting the final constellation. "The whole left side will come down on someone's head."

"My stars," Maddy said, spinning to face him, "are perfectly engineered. Unlike your personality."

"Really? Because that one's slipping." He pointed up with his champagne glass. "Though I suppose a falling star is on brand for you. Very symbolic of your events."

"Henry," Maddy said sweetly, though her eyes shot daggers at Mason, "I hope you're not too attached to your best man because I'm about two seconds away from demonstrating how lethal a Jimmy Choo can be when properly motivated."

"Careful, Chen," Mason drawled, stepping closer to adjust the allegedly crooked star himself, "threatening bodily harm at a wedding you planned isn't great for business. Though I suppose premeditated murder would give you plenty of time to work on your organizational skills in prison."

"And I'd rather paint a thousand pigeons, dye my hair green, and marry a tax attorney than admit you might occasionally be right about anything."

They were standing very close now, the star forgotten between them.

"Tax attorney?" Mason's voice dropped lower. "That's oddly specific. Been thinking about marriage a lot, Chen?"

"Only about how to make it spectacular for other people," she shot back, but her cheeks flushed pink. "Some of us create magic. Others ... exist to point out liability issues."

"Speaking of liability..." His hand brushed hers as he reached for the star. "Dance with me. Before you bring this whole place down around our ears."

"I'd rather—" she started.

"Paint a thousand pigeons?" he finished. "Yeah, I heard you the first time. Dance anyway."

To everyone's surprise, including possibly her own, Maddy did.

Henry pulled me closer as we watched them move across the floor, still bickering but with a rhythm that looked surprisingly like chemistry.

"Ten bucks says she tries to kill him before they figure it out," I murmured against his shoulder.

"Twenty says he asks her out before she gets the chance."

I looked around at my world—Mom and Dad dancing like teenagers, Victoria directing Mrs. Patterson's livestream with surprising patience, and Ivy sketching something that looked suspiciously like a bridesmaid dress. At Maddy and Mason, who'd stopped dancing to argue about whether the string quartet was playing in the right key, their faces inches apart and their eyes saying something entirely different from their words.

"Perfect," I said, and meant it. It wasn't the artificial perfect I used to chase, but the real kind—the perfectly imperfect joy of finding exactly where you belong.

Henry's arms tightened around me. "Ready for our next chapter?"

I thought about The Weathered Barn, waiting to be transformed, about all the love stories yet to unfold within its walls. How ending my career as the Breakup Broker had led to the most beautiful beginning.

"With you?" I lifted my face to his. "Always."

Above us, the stars kept falling, each glimmering as they tumbled, like tiny sparks. Behind us, Maddy's voice rose over the music—"Touch that centerpiece and die, Mason!" —followed by what sounded suspiciously like a laugh.

Because sometimes the best endings aren't endings at all —they're the first page of a much better story. And occasionally the most beautiful love stories start with someone driving you absolutely crazy.

GET A FREE BOOK.

Go to www.authorkellycollins.com

OTHER BOOKS BY KELLY COLLINS

Dive into heartwarming romance, unforgettable love stories, and second chances. Explore all of Kelly Collins' series and find your next favorite happily-ever-after! 💕

Recipes for Love

A Taste of Temptation

A Pinch of Passion

A Dash of Desire

A Cup of Compassion

A Dollop of Delight

A Layer of Love

Recipe for Love Collection 1-3

Recipe for Love Collection 4-6

The Second Chance Series

Set Free

Set Aside

Set in Stone

Set Up

Set on You

The Second Chance Series Box Set

A Pure Decadence Series

Yours to Have

Yours to Conquer

ABOUT THE AUTHOR

📚 International bestselling author of over 50 novels, Kelly Collins crafts stories that keep love alive. With a heart full of romance and a vivid imagination, she blends real-life events into captivating tales that contemporary romance, new adult, and romantic suspense fans will fall for over and over again. 💕

For More Information
www.authorkellycollins.com
kelly@authorkellycollins.com

Printed in Great Britain
by Amazon

59980020R00127